5000 DEAD DUCKS

*Lust and Revolution
in the Oilsands*

5000 DEAD DUCKS

*Lust and Revolution
in the Oilsands*

C.D. Evans and L.M. Shyba

**DURANCE VILE
PUBLICATIONS**

Durance Vile Publications Ltd.
Calgary, Alberta, Canada
www.durancevile.com
Copyright © 2011 by C.D. Evans and L.M. Shyba
All rights reserved

National Library of Canada
Cataloguing in Publications Data
Evans, C.D. and Shyba, L.M.
5000 Dead Ducks: Lust and Revolution in the Oilsands
ISBN 978-0-9689754-4-2

1. Evans C.D. (Christopher Dudley)
Shyba, L.M. (Lorene Mary)
2. Oilsands — Satire — Fiction — Alberta — Calgary

Cover Art and Illustrations by Maxwell Théroux

Author Photographs: Marcel Bitea and Lorene Shyba
Book and cover design by Lorene Shyba • Set in Minion
Printed in Canada by McAra Printing

*We dedicate this book to each other.
This experiment in collaboration has been
an experience to remember.*

THE AUTHORS

Lorene M. Shyba MFA PhD has been an international entertainment impresario, university professor, video producer, magazine publisher, advertising art director, TV talent, digital art curator, and sports car enthusiast among other things. She was the innovator of the interactive performance piece *Spies in the Oilsands* and the serious videogame *The Pipeline Pinball Energy Thrill Ride Game.* Her university affiliations have included the University of Calgary, McMaster University, and, most recently, Montana Tech of the University of Montana.

Christopher D. Evans QC practiced criminal law in Canada for forty years and is a Fellow of the American College of Trial Lawyers. He was a Bencher of the Law Society of Alberta for eight years and was appointed Queen's Counsel in 1978. He has appeared regularly as counsel at all levels of court in Alberta and NWT as well as occasional appearances in the Supreme Court of Canada. C.D. Evans' previously published titles include *Milt Harradence: The Western Flair* and *A Painful Duty: Forty Years at the Criminal Bar*

Between the wish and the thing, the world lies waiting.

— Cormac McCarthy, *All the Pretty Horses*

PART ONE

———

Tar and Feathers

———

ONE

DOCTOR MAVIS WONG screams her Jeep through the high-speed traffic roaring down from Fort Ath toward downtown Bos Taurus. Speed traps be damned. Over the noise of the frantic highway, she yells on satellite phone headset to Harold Spincter. "No! No way we could get the cannons and horns set up fast enough … duck corpses everywhere." She changes lanes to get by a convoy of transport trucks. "Yeah, flocks and frickin' flocks of 'em … banked and landed right on Pond 13, what a stinking shithole … what the devil were we supposed to do? Flap our arms? Jump up and down?" A merge and a lane weave gets her onto Elkhorn Trail. She yells at the phone, "What?! How did you find out? … What network? … Does Mailcoat know? Tell him I'll be right there … five minutes."

At the same time, JB Mailcoat, CEO of PetroFubar Energy, cracks a beer, takes a big swig and kicks his scuffed boots up on the shiny walnut desk. He surveys the corporate landscape of Bos Taurus and the mountains that stretch beyond the walls of his glass palace on the 38th floor of the PetroFubar Building. As he sucks an errant morsel of steak sandwich special from between his teeth, a succulent remnant from lunch at the Paunchmen's Club, he reflects on the pleasures of life in Bos Taurus, Alberia — fly fishing on the Blow River, Seriously Rich functions at the Egos Golf and

Country Club and invigorating chinook winds that warm up the winters. Helps that there are plenty of fellow Montexians around town to celebrate the real Thanksgiving and the Fourth of July and bring authentic yahoo and yee-haw to the annual Bos Taurus rodeo.

JB pries his thousand-mile stare off the sweeping horizon and swings his legs up and away from the top of the desk and onto the floor with a thud. A flurry of dog whines and scratches from a nest under his hobby table in the corner of the room prompts him to hurl a big rawhide bone in the direction of his black lab Slick, who lunges at it from across the Persian carpet with a rip and a salivating snort. JB reaches forward to scratch him behind the ear with a drawling mumble about huntin' season, but a rap at the door provokes a violent barkathon that knocks JB off balance, upsetting the piles of coins he had stacked up on his leather-tooled coffee table.

A muffled voice from behind the big oak door stammers, "Excuse me, JB … 2,500 dead ducks … our tailing pond—"

JB, momentarily distanced from his aura of command and control, slides around on a sea of collapsed coinage to collect his dog's collar in one swift movement. Harold Spincter opens the door a crack, saying, "a disaster."

"Whaddya *mean*, a disaster?"

Knowing from experience that Slick is nosing for a slobbering crotch sniff, or worse still cruising for an amorous leg hump, JB's Executive Assistant Harold Spincter backs into the office at a reverse trot to shore himself up between JB's mirrored bar and the beer fridge, grabbing the television remote control along the way.

"That's what she said, JB. I'm only repeating what Prime Minister Hubris—"

"Listen, Bu-ub!" JB crosses the room, square finger pointing, sleeveless vest with sweat-stains straining over his prodigious undisciplined belly, waving his can of beer. "Th' Hindenburg was a disaster. Darfur was a disaster. Fifty rigs out about five hunnerd days hittin' fifty dry holes, that's gettin' up there. This, whatever it is, ain't no disaster. This's fuck-all. Dead ducks is fuck-all!"

Punching away at the remote control, Harold says, "Yeah, I'm with you, JB." The channels flip from the twangy country music channel to JB's default favourites: the Fishing Network, ESPN, Fox News, and then a nonstop array of *Dallas* reruns. He looks up to see JB scowling. "You're pushing on an open door, JB... on a scale of one to ten, dead ducks is a minus one hundred and ninety-three." Harold, besides being a pretty good golfer and a native Bos Taurian, is a world class suckhole. "Okay," he sighs, "Here's the coverage."

JB's flatscreen springs to life with images of dead and dying ducks and a news ticker that proclaims AntiTox's discovery of yet another catastrophe. JB, true to his hard-stubble cow and oil patch roots of southwest Montexia, swings into crisis mode. "So what are you people doin' about it, tell me? Like right fuckin' now!"

MAVIS PULLS HER OLD JEEP up in front of PetroFubar, flips on the hazards lights, jumps out and catches the elevator up to the 38th Floor. Struggling to control her hammering heart, she closes her eyes and a scene from the stinking mire of muck comes flooding in. She remembers ... *the oil-soaked duck, bewildered, its eyes unfocused, trying to scream, flapping its crippled wings.* Ding. 14th Floor. *Grabbing the desperate thing, slipping and sliding in the filth, scooping it up. It didn't struggle or protest, just looked reproachful with those glazed pain-filled eyes. The poor creature flapped weakly but enough to spray ooze all over me.* Ding. 25th Floor. *Oh God, the ooze is still all over me! I wrung its neck; put it out of its agony; placed it back in the muck. What else could I do? It trembled in death.* Ding. 31th Floor. *Nimmo was out there too, pirouetting out by the busted air cannon, holding his camera up over his head to connect with the AntiTox satellite. Wanting to shout 'Nimmo, Don't rat me out. Please!!' Wanting to shout 'Sorry Nimmo. I've whored myself out to PetroFubar Energy now and now I'm in deep'.* Ding. 38th Floor.

Sliding past the inner sanctum sentinels, Mavis makes right for JB's door, maneuvering Slick's familiarity ritual with a wave of her hand and a grumble, "Ho there canine, back off." She is covered in grease, her hair pulled back with a motorcycle bandana and coveralls rolled down to her waist, exposing a tar and feather-smeared Tapperlite Folk Festival t-shirt. Slick, the dog, thunderstruck and dominated, retreats to gnaw on his rawhide.

JB spins away from the television, reeling with the twin realization that his investments in the oilsands are in jeopardy and that there is a strange, disheveled FarEast woman in the office. He yells out, "Spincter, goddammit, who the hell is this?"

Harold, tripping over his words in his haste to defuse the situation blurts out, "JB, this is Dr. Wong. She is our new environmental scientist, just joined us after three years of post-doc field work at the toxic mine pit down in Tapperlite, Montexia. Hired her to head the Environmental Science ES team. She can give you some of the ... some of the—"

"Yeah. Spit it out Bu'ub, Some of th' what?" snaps JB.

Mavis, not wanting to further embarrass Harold,

interrupts with, "Good afternoon, sir." She removes her oily glove and extends her hand but JB just glares at her. Mavis recoils her hand, using the motion as a chance to reach into her coverall pocket for her mobile which she flips to life, reciting, "According to peer-reviewed ecological data, sir, between four hundred and fifty-eight and five thousand and twenty-nine birds die each year after landing in oilsands tailings ponds rife with toxic heavy metals and acids—"

JB is, on the one hand, appalled at one so unfeminine — *like a medieval princess, no makeup, holy shit* —and, on the other, impressed by the fact that he hired someone who survived the notorious Tapperlite Superfund disaster zone. "Listen, lady, duck hunters shotgun thousands a' ducks outta' Alberia skies every year. Thass a hellava lotta feathers hittin' the deck in one year alone. A couple a' thousand gettin' a messy death? Not a big deal. And that don't include them being run down by them farmers' turbines or settin' on fancy restaurant tables or bein' turned into that there patty foize grass by planes, and what about them wind turbines?"

To control her urge to call him an asshole, Mavis contents herself with a little game of biting her tongue and picking coins up off the floor, stacking them back up onto the coffee table in what she hopes is perceived as a demonstration of cooperation.

JB isn't finished. Raising his voice to obnoxious heights he continues. "I heard wind turbines nail ten thousand birds a month. Whaddya think them AntiToxers serve at their annual piss-ups? Roast dead duck with that there l'orange, I'll betcha. Dead duck on th' rocks with a twist a' lemon. Duck a la King. Look lady, we're not talkin' about dead babies here!"

"The problem is, JB…" Harold interrupts. "The problem is that with Dr. Wong's guidance we've made dramatic improvements to our bird-deterrent system—"

"Bird-deterrent system? Fuck!" He hurls his beercan at the trash with such velocity that the office fills with an ear-splitting clang. Mavis looks over at Harold and sucks in her cheeks, hoping he interprets her exasperation.

"The problem is, JB, this new duck incident has made headlines again around the world only this time it's PetroFubar and not your competition that's between the crosshairs. Photos and videos of oil-drenched migrating fowl at Pond 13 are plastered all over the media. It's a nightmare."

"Sir, may I clarify?" Mavis realizes that Harold is making the problem worse rather than better. She recalls the list of carcinogenic polycyclic aromatics from her field notes. "Mr. President, our tailing ponds are filled with naphthalene, acenaphthylene, acenaphthene, and fluorene. The industry reports about sixty-five birds still die each year, but the fact is that the toll is much greater."

JB hisses at her with all his venom, his blood pressure pounding, "Whose side're you on anyway, lady?"

Sensing an imminent blowout of Montexian proportions, Harold grabs another beer out of the fridge, leaps over Slick, pops the can with a mollifying fizz and thrusts it between JB's wildly gesticulating arms. JB clamps the beer between his hands, raising the cool can to his lips — a gesture and smell that bring back to him sweet memories of reform school, 18-wheelers, and dirt tracks to remote well sites. He drinks deeply, his eyes reflecting a fleeting moment of calm.

Harold takes advantage of this to explain, "You may recall that at the Shareholders' Annual Meeting, questions were raised about the tailing ponds? That was when the committee of concerned shareholders suggested PetroFubar retain the services of full-time ecologists and environmentalists."

JB hurls the empty beer can, only this time it bounces off the side of the trash and hits Mavis' tower of coins, which peppers Slick with a ricochet of rebounds. The dog whimpers and slinks over to JB who croons to his dog, "Shit, sorry Slick, never made th' team." Winding up and blowing hard again, he shouts to Harold, "I don't recall any such shareholders' meeting."

"I think, in fairness, JB, you left the Annual Meeting early that day, I think that was the Northwest Territories fishing trip with Premier Svenhardt and—"

"Fuckin' A, because if I hadn't, we wouldn't be employin' no granola gropers in this man's company."

Mavis stands her ground. "May I suggest that this matter cannot be swept under the table, sir. Our press releases report that we are committed to protecting wildlife, that we are glad to discuss bird monitoring and reporting with responsible agencies, and we continue to seek better ways to protect our feathered friends —"

"Jeez, lady, gimme a break. We're in the oil business, not the Bambi and Daffy Duck and Squirrel Nutkin business." At this point, Mavis' mobile beeps but JB continues, oblivious to the interruption. "Hey, don't get me wrong, I like pets, hey, my grandkids down home got some of them birds, parrots 'er somethin', an' a cat."

Mavis checks her mobile, nodding her head as if she tolerates or, God forbid, even agrees with his ignorant opinions about Bambi and Daffy. "Sir!" Mavis exclaims, stamping her steel-toed boot and dislodging a clump of greasy mud onto JB's expensive Imperial Tabriz carpet, "Sir, more bad news since the Pond 13 ducks disaster..." JB's wincing and snorting huffs over the word 'disaster' gives her a chance to re-read the text message. "Sir, our people in the field have announced the premature deaths of some additional 2,500 ducks at our Pond 14. Another huge flock that got past the air cannons had to be euthanized."

"Euthanized? Like, offed? Twenny-five hunnerd? Is someone countin' these birds, one by one? Maybe it's one hunnerd thirty, maybe it's three thousand. Hello, I found another one: this is an ex-duck! This is a non-duck! Like I said, gimme a break."

Harold scours the flatscreen ticker tape for breaking news about the additional carnage but so far it has not hit the media. "Sir, please remember we have announced our fullest cooperation with the regulatory authorities, and are working to minimize waterfowl losses, exercising due diligence." After another quick look at the screen the anxious EA adds, "Our written press release attributes this statement to you, JB."

"Ain't I th' responsible citizen."

Harold looks at him and makes a last-ditch attempt to smooth things out, knowing his job might be on the line. "Sir, there might have been what we characterize as 'unusual bird activity' due to freezing rain in the area, which makes it difficult for the birds to fly and forces them down. They were easily approached, indicating that they were fatigued."

Mavis hides her face in her hands as JB explodes. "Jesus, Har'ld, fatigued, fat-fucking-tigued? All this energy and doo diligence and runnin' round in circles, and you've figured them birds just got rained on, tuckered out and fell outta the sky! This is what I'm payin' you for? And what about them regulators, Har'ld. I thought you got 'em pieced off."

"Trouble is, JB, the enviros are now permitted routine ride-alongs with the inspectors by the government."

"They *what*?"

Harold quails. "A not-so-bright idea of the Alberia

Minister of the Environment."

"That shithead! He wouldn't know his ass from a hole in the ground."

Mavis walks over to Harold, gives him a weary smile and takes over the television remote, cranking the volume. "Speaking of whom ... well, Mr. President, let's look at his take on the situation." The Alberia Minister of the Environment fills the screen from onsite at the Alberia oilsands. The camera pulls back to reveal a pathetic oil-covered duck, right behind the minister's talking head. "I cannot express how disappointed and frustrated I am that this regrettable incident occurred," he intones, reading with poppy eyes from the teleprompt, "Alberians deserve answers to why this happened again, and we will do everything we can to get these answers quickly."

"Whose side are these pricks on?" JB snorts. "Who voted for these arseholes? Who donated to them?"

The Honourable Minister continues: "Provincial officials ensure that PetroFubar is preventing further flocks of birds from landing. Air cannons are said to be operating, but their deployment has been sporadic and dilatory. Premier Svenhardt has called the situation aggravating and frustrating, and questions whether the deterrents were in place—"

"Sporadic... and what? You fuckin' prick! Turn that prick off."

"Sir," lectures Mavis, "it is a feather in our cap that we are addressing these concerns." She relays a half-truth that gives her moral compass a spin. "Indeed, we have deployed extra air cannons, flare guns and air horns to try to scare the birds away, but with no luck so far, I'm afraid. The Athabauna valley is a busy migrating route for waterfowl."

"You're afraid? I ain't afraid. I want this problem and

this shower a' shit publicity squashed, right now. As for the freezin' rain, how 'bout gettin' a new God? Old one's worn out."

"JB", says Harold, "enviros are calling the oilsands a duck killing ground, it's getting a lot of media play, and it's catching on everywhere. The party line is that all PetroFubar and the other operators get is a slap on the wrist. You know who is getting a lot of mileage out of this, eh? AntiTox."

Mavis, remembering the sighting of Nimmo at Pond 13, jumps at the chance to change the subject but just makes things worse, "…and AntiTox says the government is just a public relations firm for the tar sands."

"The *what*?"

"Sorry, Sir, I meant oilsands, of course."

"You bin brain-fucked like them AntiTox stoops, lady?"

She flinches at his insult. "If I may express urgency, sir, credible ecological research is postulating that the number of bird deaths in the Alberia tar sands — oilsands, I mean, of course — tailing ponds is between seven and seventy-seven times higher than our own energy industry estimates."

"Pustulating. Ya' mean like pimples?" JB tilts back his head and roars a laugh at his pun, waking up his sleeping dog who leaps up and sniffs around for a place to relieve himself. Mavis, speaking out over Slick's pathetic whining, says, "Sir, our industry reported an average sixty-five birds die each year. However, according to ecological data, as many as 10,029 birds expire each year from landing in tailing ponds rife with toxic heavy metals and acids—"

"So it's 10,000 dead ducks now, plus 29, huh? Sixty-five a year sounds about right to me." He laughs again and walks over to the door, leading Slick by the scruff of the neck and boots him out into the hall so his toilet needs become someone else's problem. Then he shuffles over to the fridge to grab another beer. For some strange reason, he thinks of offering one to Mavis but is stopped by what he considers to be the dumbest idea he's ever heard.

"Sir, we must emphasize that we are committed to protecting wildlife. I suggest that PetroFubar support me in the establishment of a bigger research team. We'll visit the field in a scientifically defensible manner to erect deterrents, to assess the number of birds dying, and to release the results in a timely manner."

"Scientifically defensible? Har'ld, what the hell—?"

"Perhaps, JB, we might excuse Dr. Wong at this time, with our thanks, and we can consult further after she has had a chance to explore our corporate options in consultation with her colleagues on staff." He nods at Mavis to beat a hasty retreat.

"Yeah, Har'ld, whatever. How many of these people are we payin'?"

Mavis, glad to be out of there knowing that her Jeep's blinking hazard lights are going to burn out her battery, exits JB's office with bad grace, stomping off more clumps of oily mud as she leaves.

"Who hired that drab?"

"It's a different world, JB," explains Harold as he runs around the office scooping up Mavis' leftover mud chunks with a wadded up Bos Taurus newspaper. "We have to keep up with the times, and times are changing."

"Oh, thass real original, Bu'ub! What the hell…? Who the hell…? How'd this get out, ennaways? I mean, ain't we got folks that we hire to catch these things, like, they find some dead ducks, they get rid of 'em. Thass what we pay people for, good money."

"The problem is, JB—"

"Stop sayin' the 'problem is', Har'ld. Try saying' the 'solution is' for a change.'"

JB leaves Harold to ponder this order, returns to the fridge and in a great and unusual show of camaraderie, tosses Harold a beer, causing Harold to squirm with a warm and fuzzy sense of belonging. JB belches and points at a plush leather chair and Harold sits down. JB plops himself into another chair and drums his fingers in a staccato fashion on the coffee table. While JB leans forward to assemble the fallen coin castle, Harold unravels the backstory of the enviro ride-alongs.

"JB, sometime back the provincial government told oil-sands companies that they had to allow reasonable access by NGOs and private environmental groups like AntiTox so their people can monitor avian and animal mortality at our facilities. This permits them to walk the perimeters of our tailing ponds so they can observe how many birds are landing in the ponds and estimating the percentage that die—"

"They do what? That's private property, Bu'ub!"

"...then they multiply those numbers by the number of tailing ponds we have." Harold purses his lips and takes a small sip of the strong beer. "It *is* a problem, JB, a big problem." JB scowls and leans forward, jingling a pocket full of coins while Harold continues. "I guess the solution is, we're going to have to get Mavis some more people and a better system. Our bird-deterrent team is understaffed and it's ill-equipped. They don't have enough cannons, flares, and horns all around the waste ponds, and some of these are twelve kilometres, er eight miles, square. Employees are complaining that they have only one truck to transport the rousting devices, and no company boats, and one of them must have blabbed to AntiTox. But the fact is, our Mavis didn't have the people to set up a deterrent system soon enough and quick enough."

"You mean they were sittin' around on their fat arses drinkin' coffee and playin' cards. Fire all the fuckers."

"JB, I mean to say, look, this is a big public humiliation for us and for the other oilsands operators. Like I said, dead ducks have made headlines around the world. And now the environuts are yelling for the government's heads as well for what they say is failing to oversee the oilsands operations. Nimmo Vandam, one of the AntiTox activists, says that tailing ponds violate federal law protecting migratory birds, and is arguing that the oilsands industry is derelict."

JB sits back in his chair, silent.

"The provincial government opposition are also on this big time: their leader, Fabiola Monk, has expressed anger, calls the provincial government 'gutless', and likens the situation to the oil spill off the Montexia coast."

"Jeez, that's another stupid socialist commie. Sure, bring up the coast oil spill. Barf it up all over th' GD place."

"You should know that the province and the feds are both laying charges against PetroFubar."

"Ain't that what they call double jeopardy?" JB is no fool.

"The province charges under the Environmental Protection Act: failing to prevent hazardous substances from coming into contact with wildlife—"

"So, get th' lawyers to plead that the ducks ran at them substances with their beaks, or somethin.'"

"The feds charge under the Migratory Birds Convention Act, for depositing a harmful substance in waters frequented by migratory birds."

"Birds have conventions? Tell 'em next year to go to Vegas."

JB belches, drains the remainder of his beer and saunters over to his hobby table. "Har'ld, you value your job, you get onto this thing, and you make it go away. You get me, Bu'ub? I'm wearied of this shit. Make it go away. Now." He points a big square finger at the door. He picks up the duck-hunting decoy he is almost finished whittling. "This is the only kind of dead duck deserves our attention from hereon in, get it?"

Harold looks around for a place to put his half-empty beer can and settles on the coffee table, adding to JB's reconstructed array of coins and now, even dog biscuits. His chair gives an embarrassing squeaky fart as he rises and he makes his way over to JB's big oak door, stepping across the threshold carefully to avoid Slick's ballistic re-entry into the room.

JB meanwhile swivels around in his chair, focusing his scowling attention on the daily market on the flatscreen. He mumbles to himself, "Dow ... TSX ... price of oil, the price of gold .... Gold's up, big." Then, to Slick, his confidant and companion he adds, "Well, boy, what we got here is the price of everythin' and the value of nothin'." Then, the ticker tape on the screen shows the carnage has been upped to 5,000 dead ducks. A disaster.

FIRST THING the next day, JB presides at PetroFubar's opulent boardroom in tense consultation with the bright lights of the legal department, ameliorated by the expensive attendance of Donald Grandstander QC, the hired gun from The Big Firm.

The Oracle, *at $600 bucks an hour,* notes JB, clears his throat to enable the full resonance of his plum tones.

"Mr. President, an international coalition of environmental groups has launched a successful public relations offensive against what they characterize as our 'dirty oil'."

Grinding his teeth, JB spits and shouts, "Show me enny oil that ain't grease black dirty, counsellor. Where've these assholes bin?"

Grandstander, feigning patience, explains, "In the talk show studios of the world, for one venue. The environmental groups are expert media manipulators. AntiTox is only one of the more than a dozen groups engaged in effective lobbying campaigns. This is meant to convince the Montexian president and congress not to shelter the carbon intensive oilsands against draconian climate-change and greenhouse gas regulations."

Grandstander stops to sip coffee and to survey JB's level of comprehension. He continues slowly, knowing that the longer he takes, the bigger the bill. "Carbon regulations are impossible to achieve. Witness the international conference debacles. But the delegates all agree on one slogan: 'Don't buy Alberia's dirty oil'. More ominously, these same manipulators are meeting welcoming arms in the Candidian capital."

"Another bunch of fairies," grumbles JB. "What country in the world would allow a coalition of ragtag commies and them trendy liberal left-wingers to pitch out the elected government? An' don't forget, Grandstander, altho' a lot of their campaignin' is filtered through th' perfeshnal environuts, it's sure as hell being financed by them other high-producin' countries. They're the ones what wanna shut down our sands production. We're sitting on th' second largest oil reserves on the planet, and we don't give 'em sweet dreams."

"Mr. President," says Grandstander, "extracting the bitumen produces about three times as many emissions per barrel compared to what is called conventional oil. Our Candidian federal government has seized upon that—"

"What da they want to do, shoot themselves in the head?

Out in these parts, they already shot themselves in the foot!"
"Every kick in the balls of an Alberian resident, Mr.
President, buys the Coalition ten Eastern votes from the two
most populous provinces. And the two most populous provinces are always looking down south. What the Montexians
are wrestling with right now is whether they want 'clean'
oil from dirty oligarchies run by unsound, umm, persons,
or do they want 'dirty' oil from a clean regime? And they're
wrestling with this because their nation is quintessentially
gas guzzlers and suburban sprawl. They will never get the oil
usage down, it's just going to go up. They also want conti-
nental energy self-sufficiency, which they would get with our
vast oilsands potential production. But enviros, like AntiTox
and their fellow travellers, have got one big toehold into
Montexian politicians."

"Montexians guzzle over fourteen million barrels a oil a
day, Grandstander, an' seventy per cent a that is imported.
Well, fuck 'em, we'll sell our product to FarEast — to the
highest bidders. We'll ship it through pipelines to the ports.
And I'll tell you this, any stuff we ship to Candidia's west
coast is gonna be bought by Montexians anyway or by
brokers who'll resell it back to them."

Burke, PetroFubar's senior lawyer, thinks he had better
chime in at this point: "JB, we do have a credible story to tell
the world, about responsible development of the oilsands—"

"Jesus, Bu'ub, what planet're you on ennaways, we're in
resource development. I said already, twenty times! Not PR.
We work for the shareholders, not the little folks."

Harold, who has been studying JB's style of rhetoric,
political values and mannerisms for years, sees his opening:
"The problem is, er," he stammers, then stands and jingles
coinage in his pocket for courage, raising his voice to

Mailcoatian decibel levels, "the problem is the goddamn provincial government. They haven't taken time yet to get oilsands policies and communication strategy in line." He thumps his fist. "We're talking about the future of billions of dollars of PetroFubar investment, but Alberia politicians are sittin' on their hands." He looks around and his face goes red.

JB nods and grunts in agreement, a gesture that induces, in Harold, an orgasmic thrill. JB drives home the point, "Them farmers don't know their arse from their elbow, sittin' on their butts countin' ever day to th' pension. We elected them suckers to manage this resource. They couldn't pour piss out of a cowboy boot if the instructions were written on the heel." JB pauses to allow Harold the pleasure of leading a chorus of suckhole-forced simpering laughter to ring out around the table. "Provincial politicians ain't doing fuck-all. Time to throw th' fuckers out."

Certain ineluctable forces turn JB's crank. One priority item is unrivalled global capitalism with a concomitant priority of a government at the beck and call of PetroFubar Energy's needs. "Well, screw 'em. We'll shut down th' shipments to Montexia, that'll put th' squeeze on them sons of bitches, and we'll pipe it straight out to th' west coast an' sell it to th' FarEasters—"

Grandstander holds up his hand with that annoying movement that always irritates JB. "There may be some hair on that, Mr. President." He pauses. "Prime Minister Hubris has already stated that the feds will withhold construction permits for any such proposed pipeline."

"She what? Who th' hell—? "

"... does she think she is? Well, the Prime Minister of Candidia, to start."

"Which Candidia you talkin' about? Jeez, did you fuckers

win on the Plains a' Abraham or what?" Sneezing over everyone within range, and wiping his dripping nose with his sleeve. "Goddamnit, Burke, walk us through this. What permits?"

Burke says, "Under the National Pipelines Act, JB, the federal government has to approve inter-provincial transportation of carbon constituents—"

"Them Eastern bastards're gonna tell us we cain't pipe our product across Candidia to sell to the FarEasters, or whoever? Listen up, we got the parties, we got the partners, we got the financing, we got the volume guarantee from the other producers, it's all systems go—"

Burke responds, "That's not all, Mr. President." He checks his mobile. "We just got word that the Montexian government has refused the permit for our proposed new high-capacity bitumen pipeline."

JB pounds his fist on the table and stands up in a display of urgency. "Well, that's the last straw. Provincial politicians ain't doing fuck-all to protect our industry from the feds. Time to throw th' fuckers out. We're just not gonna take this shit, I'm tellin' you right' now! In Candidia Francis they got one million separatists with ten cents each. In Alberia, we got seven separatists with a hundred million bucks each. You're sittin' wit one a them."

He takes time to stare down every set of eyes around the big oak table. Nobody says a thing.

"Har'ld, get that asshole Fred Fiddler on the line. Time for him to walk his separatist talk!"

"You're sure you want to get into bed with that megalomaniac Fiddler?" Grandstander asks, having more than once been privy to Fiddler's Napoleon complex.

JB, with a mission-from-God determination in his voice

shouts out, "He's the only megalo-whatever we got. Har'ld, get that asshole Fiddler on th' line. Right fuckin' now."

TWO

FRED FIDDLER, Queen's Counsel, Fellow of the Montexian College of Trial Lawyers, barrister-at-law, Leader of the Criminal Bar, preens as he stands before the full-length mirror in the Gentlemen Barristers Robing Room. He admires his swallow-tailed QC court coat that, together with his new silk gown, he has acquired in London from Ode and Ravenshill, Gentleman Tailors and Robemakers to, among others, the Lord Chancellor and Fred Fiddler. Displayed with Lord Hailsham's trousers in a glass display case is an invitation to Lord Nelson's funeral. These sorts of symbols are all-important to Fred Fiddler

Fred is to address the jury in a routine murder. Not a big deal. Two louts got into consensual fisticuffs; one of their number did not get up. So the case has got some problems for the prosecution. The surviving lout's dad has some bucks and retains the famous criminal lawyer. And the famous criminal lawyer is examining his aquiline phizzog in the glass, because he is as vain as a man who is the centre of his own universe can be, and he is Hollywood handsome and, as his law partner Walt Semchuk would say, Hollywood vacant. Fred is appreciating, as he always does, his dark, brilliantined hair and his blue eyes that can be limpid and even kind, but can turn to the piercing cold steel-grey of the master cross-examiner.

His strong mouth transposes with alacrity from a winning smile to a deprecating sneer, this patented trademark sneer practiced by Fred in the mirror. Fred is a master thespian; his whole life is an act; he is, he perceives, destined for great things. Fred hungers for political office, any political office, for capital "R" Recognition, and beyond mere recognition for the adulation of others. He yearns to be worshipped. Fred the Great!

Fred is an effective criminal defence counsel, a prince of the profession towering over colleagues less gifted. It is not that Fred is any good, observes Walt Semchuk, it is just that the others are so bad. Lost in self-love — Fiddler is, as Cicero observed, a lover of himself without a rival — Fred recovers himself at the urgent vibration of the mobile strapped to his hip like a Buntline special.

"Yes. Fiddler here, barrister at law."

"Mr. Fiddler, my name is Harold Spincter—"

His caller is interrupted. "Yes. You may wish to call my secretary and speak to her." The barrister-at-law adds, "I'm in trial."

"Mr. Fiddler, I am the executive assistant to JB Mailcoat of PetroFubar Energy Inc—"

Fred does a double take. "Did you say 'JB Mailcoat'?"

"Yes, Mr. Fiddler."

"*The* JB Mailcoat?" Fred Fiddler's naiveté sometimes shows through his veneer of sophistication.

"There is only one, Mr. Fiddler."

Some of the recipients of that intelligence might breathe *thank God!* Fred Fiddler reacts as if shocked with a Taser in his gut. "Yes, um, well, umm—"

"Mr. Fiddler, Mr. Mailcoat is well aware of your formidable reputation, sir, and is a great admirer of yours."

"Well, that's very—" Fred, the professional wordsmith, can't think of an appropriate word. He thinks, *JB Mailcoat!*

"Mr. Fiddler, Mr. Mailcoat would like you to join him for luncheon. He wishes to consult with you on a matter of grave importance, in which you may have common ground. He suggests the Fossil Fuel Club. What would be an agreeable day and time for you?" Pause. "There is some urgency."

"Yes, of course. Well, say, uh… let's see, I'll have a jury out later today, but — assuming they have a verdict before noon tomorrow — how about lunch?"

"Most satisfactory, Mr. Fiddler. May I give you a contact number should you still be engaged in court?"

"Yes, engaged in combat, that is my calling. A good idea. Yes."

Harold supplies the number. "Thank you, Mr. Fiddler. Mr. Mailcoat looks forward to your meeting tomorrow."

"As do I. Thank you, Mr.…uh—"

"Spincter. Harold Spincter. Good afternoon, Mr. Fiddler."

Fred Fiddler takes the noisy, dark courthouse fire escape stairs two at a time, all the way to the fourth floor and not missing a beat. He encounters his long-time criminal law associate Walt Semchuk, who is sitting on the fourth floor landing, sucking on a ripe, juicy plum and reading his trial brief.

Fiddler explodes, "This is the big one, Semchuk! This is the big one!"

Walt Semchuk eyes his partner Fred Fiddler, spits the plum pit into the corner of the stairwell and wipes plum juice off his chin with a Jolly Roger bandana. "No need for emotion so early in the day," he says in his cold, smooth voice. "Slow down, Fred."

"Walt, I just got the call. The call!"

Walt stuffs the bandana into his pocket. "The call of the wild? Yes, I think I got that part, Fred. What's the next part?"

"JB Mailcoat, President and Chief Executive Officer of PetroFubar Energy Inc."

"A tedious fraud and an ignoramus."

Fred says, "Park your opinions, Walt. We're talking big money here. Money and power. We're on the way! We're taking Alberia out!"

"First things first, perhaps. Did he say why he got in touch with you?" Looking up and noting Fred's vacant expression, he continues. "I thought not. It may be about a speeding ticket. JB is overbearing." Walt ponders as he imagines the prospect of sending big bills to the notorious JB Mailcoat. *And seriously rich and well-connected.* His thoughts race headlong into his dreams of revolution ... *and may be appropriate for our purposes.*

He unfolds his lanky form. It is a given that Walt dominates Fred. He always speaks to him as to a child. He pulls Fred's strings. "Listen up Fred," he says, "if it is the big one, go for it." Before Fred can react to Walt's suggestions, they are interrupted by a learned junior bursting into the fire-exit stairwell, agitated and out of countenance as well as out of breath. "Mr. Fiddler, I've been looking all over for you. The judge is waiting."

"Tell him to fucking wait." What is the use of being a senior counsel if one does not upbraid the odd jumped-up judge? His junior disappears, looking worried, knowing that he will bear the brunt of the judge's displeasure. Fred poses like a comic Balzac character. "Yes. I have to take Alberia out."

"That's 'we,' Fred. You can't do it without me and you know it."

"Yes. That's true."

As they part company, Walt gives one last conspiratorial order in Fiddler's left ear. "Keep saying to yourself, remember this is the Big One." Walt smiles his diabolical half smile, disengaging Fiddler with a ol' boys slap on the back and says, "I'm off to the courtroom to make a pretense of a defence if I can't plead out my puke."

Fiddler explodes. "This is the Big One, Semchuk! This is the Big One!"

Walt Semchuk, Fred Fiddler's partner and puppetmaster, is handsome with elegant, curvaceous eyebrows and piercing grey eyes. He collects precious minerals and does his best work at night. He appreciates the work of the Dutch masters, listens to Baroque music and is good at manipulating people. He was born Vladimir Semchuk in Northern Alberia, but the rig hands on his summer oilpatch job between semesters at the University of Alberia law school elevated his name to Vlad when they suspected he was hanging upside down in tree branches during break. In his early career after law school, he was a prosecutor, and in that position he learned the essence of effective advocacy — knowing when to keep his mouth shut. As he had the ability to make up his mind at once and was intelligent, he spent no time at all preparing his cases. He could do them off the top of his head with simply a charge sheet in his hand. After five years, he had learned his trade, terminated his office, and went into private practice. He was snapped up by the criminal law firm of Fiddler and Associates.

Today, while Fiddler addresses his murder jury, JB whittles at his duck decoy, Mavis Wong updates the PetroFubar Community Development website, and Harold rides up and down the elevator to the soothing sound of his favourite muzak, Walt defends the accused murderer Bertrand Doof, who offed his spouse with a roofing hammer then gave the cops a free and voluntary confession. The Assistant Chief Medical Examiner is on the stand, the prosecutor extracting the causes and mechanisms of the victim's abrupt and unanticipated death.

Walt has read the autopsy report and has no questions of this expert witness. Anyone stupid enough to question an experienced medical examiner in a homicide where the causes and mechanisms of death are obvious is an idiot. One also gets a brownie point from the court for refraining. He replaces the toothpick in his mouth and reopens his tabloid newspaper at the financial pages. The trial proceeds.

After the close of evidence, Walt rises to address a jury composed of what he terms, with his trademark contempt, *twelve National Enquirer readers.*

"May it please Your Lordship. Ladies and Gentlemen," Walt gives his address, brief and to the point, then sits down. The jury is out for less than an hour, and returns with a verdict of guilty, a foregone conclusion. Following penalty submissions, his client getting the mandatory life and no parole for ten years, his client cries out to him from the prisoner's dock, "What happens to me now, Mr Semchuk?"

"Well," says Walt, "the good news is, you'll have a place to stay; the bad news is, you'll have to get used to the company of strangers."

Clang.

AT LUNCHEON at the Fossil Fuel Club, JB and Fred have passed on the dessert tray and are concentrating on more cocktails. For Fred Fiddler QC, the talk has been stimulating to this point. Fred is emboldened by the conjured flattery of

JB Mailcoat, the elaborate meaningless niceties larding the president's considered obsequies, however insincere. Fred is heady with visions of public adulation. He has subjected JB to the full range of his patented trade-craft 'engaged' facial expressions and shoulder gestures: the narrowing of the eyes to signify astute appreciation of the president's point, also used in court as an ominous response to some quackery from a frightened witness, thus the technique polished over years, as with his other 'expressions'; the narrowing of the eyes in the 'appreciation' phase shown by a deliberate firm down-turned setting of the mouth and hunching of the shoulders, denoting strength — strength of character, physical strength, stamina, being up to the job; the self-deprecating smile with the murmur of a suppressed chuckle, to respond to the effusive compliments with which JB has peppered his remarks to this point; the terrible scowl along with a shaking, trembling of the shoulders suffusing an aggressive visage which Fred has worked on in front of the mirror for years; the sonorous repetition of his trademark 'Yes' with nodding head, demonstrating that he is *ad idem* with his interlocutor. Most telling are the piercing eyes and pointing finger gambit when thrusting home an 'important point', however banal and absurd.

"How th' hell ... look, Fred, I'm an old cowhand, and I like yer Rio Grande, so let's make it 'Fred' and 'JB', whadda ya' say?"

The self-deprecating, disarming smile: "Why, Mr. President, I'd be honoured, sir."

"JB it is, Fred, from now, ya hear!" JB calls over the waiter and orders another Lagavulin single malt, on the rocks. "Want another Old Fashioned, Fred?" Fred responds with a request for an Amaretto Delight. JB chortles to himself and tells the waiter, "Put an umbrella in it too, will ya."

CD EVANS AND LM SHYBA

Back on track with the revolution, JB asks, "Fred, how did the Candidian gov'mint get so fucked up? I don't get the politics in this country. Down home in Montexia, like, there's two parties, that's th' choice, black an' white. Th' country is polarized, okay, but the system works, Fred. Folks goes one way or tother, they's lefty-commies or the Christian right, but it's also all them checks and balances and advise and consent, and it works out fine. An' the balance of power rests with the Montexian States."

Piercing eyes ploy, pointing finger: "Yes. As it should be, JB. Candidia is a confederation of dunces." With his trademark sneer, Fred launches in. "Let me give you the contrast to our Alberia advantage. West over the mountains? That's the biggest open-air insane asylum in the Western world. The prairie provinces, you die of boredom just passing through." Fred's voice is loud and the group at the next table nod their heads. "Any place east is just a foreign country! And east of the east just a bunch of people on the dole." A couple at another table say "Right on, man."

JB responds, "Me and my rich oilpatch buds, we'll be your money muscle 'cuz we just mine this joint like Jupiter's moon, make a pile, leave a mess, who gives a shit, and then, get th' hell out and go back to God's country." JB figures he's come on a bit strong but knows that's what this asshole Fiddler wants to hear.

Fred raises his trembling, pointing finger. "The greatest outrage, Mr. President, is the federal government, a coalition of lefty libs and socialist-commies and they displace an elected party. This puppet prime minister they put in, Gabrielle Hubris, is bad news for the oilsands. We cannot continue this way in this country. Development of the oilsands is in peril."

"This may be just what we bin waitin' for, Bu'ub...I mean, Fred." JB shakes his big head and wipes his glasses with the bottom of his tie. "I still don't get it, how could this happen?"

"JB, under our constitution, and according to constitutional law, it was legal for the Governor General to allow the coalition to form a government."

"Geez, Fred, you need a new constitution."

Eyes narrow. "That has crossed my mind, Mr. President."

"You know, Fred, I bin thinkin', I bin thinkin' a lot about this, th' only way to stop the flow of negative press about the 5,000 dead ducks and get the attention of all them Eastern assholes—"

Fred is galvanized. He trembles and quakes like he's in the throes of a divine intervention. "Yes!" he leaps from his chair, the umbrella-clad drink spilling hither and yon, his voice rising multiple decibels, "We've got no choice!" The trademark puffing out of the cheeks to accompany the practiced terrible scowl. "We're taking Alberia Out!" The Fossil Fuel Club explodes with cheers and applause from the other oil patch diners.

JB, buoyed by the huge show of support says, "Okay, Fred, do it. Just do it. Don' worry none 'bout th' money. Thass all in hand. Thass all taken care of. All the money ya want, all the money ya need."

Narrowed eyes. "Mr. President, this is big. We're on our way."

"Yeh, Fred, an' I'll drink to that." JB bellows across the dining room. "Hey, waiter! Don' jus' stand there with yer finger up. Replace this man's drink and bring me a double Lagavulin. An' move with a purpose, I'm payin' your salary, Bu'ub!"

THREE

A T six P.M. as a result of information received, Staff
Sergeant Augustus Boot, Police Service Special Task
Force, in company with Detective Constable First Class
Roland Hegarty and a nervous hotel manager, arrive at the
door to Suite 69 at the Dilettante Hotel. The Constable moves
to knock. "No," hisses Boot, and nods to the manager who
fumbles with a ring of keys and presents a passkey to the
Constable with a trembling hand. Hegarty inserts the key
into the lock and gives it a half twist to the left. "Not double-
locked," he whispers. Boot draws his sidearm, the manager
shrinks back against the wall. "Please," he raises his hands,
"No blood. The rooms have just been redecor—"

Celeste Kinderman QC, senior partner of one of the more
omnipotent law firms, Burwash Kinderman, and Professor
Ursula Vere, tenured Law Professor at the University of Bos
Taurus and participating associate at Burwash Kinderman
are splayed out on the four-poster bed, giggling and squealing in a belly-to-belly lickfest of girl action. Celeste's power
suit has been unbuttoned and unzipped at strategic locations,
exposing her ample breasts which bobble around like sailing
buoys as the women roll around in frolicking laughter. The
svelte Professor Vere has a one-piece spandex dress rolled
both up and down, exposing her lace strapless bra on one

end and her soft little satin garter belt on the other. The dress forms a cinch around her waist that Celeste grabs onto while she spanks Ursula's round, soft-but-firm ass, an action that provokes a delighted shriek. Both women have silk fishnet stockings on their heads, pulled down so that the filigree lace of the stocking tops make them look like pirates ready to plunder riches, which really they are and have been in many more ways than this.

"What is that annoying scritchy-scratchy noisy noise?" purrs Celeste to Ursula, annoyed.

"Police!" cry Boot and Hegarty, as they hit the door simultaneously, which yields but two inches before the night chain, fortuitously latched, brings it and the two coppers into sharp contact. The bunco squad put their combined weight upon the door, the chain gives way, and they both spill into the room, collapsing like clowns at an ice show.

Ursula pauses in her ministrations, lifts her magnificent, stocking-clad head, but continues to stroke Celeste's dimpled thigh with one hand even as she brushes her massive dark tresses back with the other. "What do you want, you idiots?" she purrs. "This is a private room."

Staff Sergeant Boot gets to his feet, holsters his snubnosed issue revolver, produces the Warrant to Search, and begins to read, eyes averted, "Whereas the complainant has reasonable and probable grounds —"

While Boot drones on and on, Celeste and Ursula zip, button, roll up and roll down spandex and make themselves respectable except for the fishnet pirate headgear that, as a climax to their affair, they remove from the crowns of each others' heads with slow murmurs of affection and sighs that can only be described as an orgasm of silk and lace. Constable Hegarty shuffles around, snatching peeks of the beautiful

Ursula Vere between phrases of Boot's search warrant speech. He proffers his wallet badge followed by a quiet ribboning of police yellow marking tape about the bed crying out, "This area is a crime scene!" Hegarty then goes to the telephone, lifts the receiver, and speaks: "Constable Hegarty, Special Task Force. Do you read?" Pause. He nods and hangs up.

"Blast!" mutters Celeste to Ursula, more as a sigh than an expletive. "The Ordland phone call has been monitored." Celeste Kinderman QC has a lot to lose. Fifty-two years old, she is youngest personal lawyer to have served the Premier of Alberia and, of course, the first woman to fill the much-sought-after role. Senior corporate partner of Burwash Kinderman, a senior Bencher of The Law Society of Alberia, and the powerful chair of its pompous discipline committee, she also made it onto the list of *Bos Taurus* magazine's Top Ten hottest butch lesbians in Alberia by blowing the other contestants away in the category of pertness of nipples. Celeste is legally married to Flossy Megadoll, the house singer at the Fizzique club, who is every bit as femme as Celeste is butch, herself having appeared in *Bos Taurus* magazine with her Cinderella slipper collection. Celeste is not at all concerned about her wife's reaction to this sumptuous extramarital liaison as they have what might be considered an open marriage, but is mortified that there might be a leak in the dyke about her much more dangerous liaisons with Ordland, gold and offshore money stashes.

Boot fishes in his breast pocket for the plastic-coated police warning and reads the usual claptrap aloud: "Mrs. Kinderman, you may be charged with a serious criminal offence. Do you wish to say anything in answer to the charge? You are not obliged to say anything, but anything you do say may be taken down and used in evidence—"

Celeste butts in, "Am I under arrest?"

"No, ma'am, not at this time."

"Am I charged?"

"No, ma'am, not at this time."

"What are the allegations against me?"

"Eleven counts of fraud and theft, ma'am, with respect to the Heritage Trust Fund of the Province of Alberia."

Hegarty starts removing papers from the table and places them in a large briefcase.

"Ursula," shouts Celeste as she notes Hegarty seizing an essential stack of correspondence, "Call up Mr. Fred Fiddler at the firm of...umm... well, Fiddler and Associates ... immediately."

"Phone him your-fucking-self, darling. You'll do fine." She inspects her elegant fishnets for snags and fluids and folds them into a special suede-lined compartment in her bejeweled handbag.

Turning to Boot, Celeste gains her composure, fishes a plastic-coated card from her own wallet and reads, with admirable presence of mind, "I wish to consult counsel. I have nothing more to say at this time."

WALT'S COINCIDENTAL FANTASY about voluptuous women in a rollicking sexual encounter is shattered by the urgency of the phone ringing on his office desk — a jangling intrusion which he regards always with distaste. *Oh well, he thinks, as he reaches for it, maybe it's a client with money and in trouble.*

Ingrid comes on the line from the outer office. She screens all of his calls. The price of Semchuk's freedom is her eternal vigilance. "It's Mrs. Celeste Kinderman."

"Celeste Kinderman? That stuck-up corporate bitch.

What does she want with the likes of me, do you suppose?"

"She is calling for Fred, but Fred's still out, probably with Mr. Mailcoat. I told her you were his partner." Ingrid pauses, still hoping Walt will take the call. "Maybe she stole a million dollars."

"She's likely on a Law Society inquisition of Fred's latest heresy. Well, put her through."

"Mr. Fiddler—?" breathes the calm female voice on the other end of the line.

"I'm his partner, Walt Semchuk. Mr. Fiddler is out and about, swanning with the swells, otherwise engaged."

'It's Celeste Kinderman. I should like to retain your firm's professional services. Forthwith."

"Yes?"

"You and, of course, Mr. Fiddler. I am at the Dilettante Hotel, room 69. There are some gentlemen here who have a warrant to search these premises. I think it important you might get here right away."

"What gentlemen?"

"A Sergeant...uhh, ooh, one moment Mr....uhh...is it Sunchuk—"

"Semchuk. Walt Semchuk."

"He's giving me his card. Staff Sergeant Augustus Boot, ummm, Police Service."

Boot of the Yard! No lightweight. "Put him on the blower," Semchuk orders.

"Mr. Fiddler...oh, Mr. Semchuk. How're you?"

"Is there anybody on this line, Sergeant? Except the bug, I mean."

"No, sir."

"Staff...Augi...are you nuts? That's Premier Svenhardt's lawyer you're purporting to arrest. She's got a direct pipeline to God. Whatever she's done, she didn't do it."

The Staff Sergeant plays it cool at his end. "Several allegations of fraud and theft, Mr. Semchuk. Yes, sir. We have a search warrant, sir, yes, in proper order, sir."

Good old Augi, making him look good to his putative client. "Who else is there?"

"Constable Hegarty, sir, and a lady of possible questionable reputation, a Miss —"

Walt hears an assertive female voice yelling corrections to him in the background. "A Mrs. ... sorry"… more derisive instructions from Ursula— "a *Professor* Vere, sir."

"Is she under arrest? You know, Augi, it's still not a crime in this country to fuck your colleague, if that's who she is, and what this is."

"Professor Vere is Mrs. Kinderman's, er, mistress, sir, so to speak. Not under arrest at this time."

Walt wants to ask him if he saw any of the fun but thinks better of it, instead saying, "Put her on, will you."

"I'd like to, sir," Augustus Boot says with a dry chuckle, "but I'm not sure if she hits for our team."

THE EVENING SUN wafts into Walt's spartan office and by now Walt feels the effects of heat of both kinds, the rising temperature in the room and the warm, lusty thoughts of *flagrente dilecto* in room 69 of the Dilettante Hotel, just around the corner. While waiting for the mysterious Professor Vere to come on the line, he stands up and squirms out of his suit jacket, adjusts the rise in his trousers, closes the blinds and cracks open the window. Fred Fiddler's stuffed sharks, suspended from the ceiling, sway in the breeze out in the lobby, casting dancing shadows across Fred's framed photos of himself with every pomposity and social climber who was ever anybody in Bos Taurus politics or society.

Ursula Vere comes on the line with a breathy salutation and before she can say anything more, Walt warns her, "Now, listen to me. This is being recorded. You may be a prosecution witness. I may be Mrs. Kinderman's lawyer. You don't have to speak to me if you don't want to."

"Thank you, go ahead, Mr. Semchuk," Ursula says.

"If the police want to call you as a witness, they have to give you a subpoena. You are entitled to independent legal advice before you speak with them. Under oath, of course. *Capiche*?"

"I understand," and then she puts Celeste back on the line.

"Mr. Fiddler—"

"Mr. Semchuk. Mrs. Kinderman, whatever you have said or want to say, shut up. Volunteer nothing. Answer no questions. I'm on the way over. What room number again? All right. I'm on the way. Belt up."

THE DILETTANTE IS AN OLD railroad hotel of cowboy rococo façade that has seen better days, but still commands a certain aura of decayed elegance with the Bos Taurus *cognoscenti*. It is, for example, a popular locale for Law Society dinners. The elevators have large brass-fronted doors, and funny 1920s floor pointers above them, and they are still run by wizened pensioners.

"Floor, please."

"Wherever room 69 is."

"That would be the seventeenth. They are nice rooms."

"I'm sure."

Room 69 would be one of the posher suites, on the floor

below the Penthouse, scene of Walt's only wedding reception, his first and last in fact. He had never got to it, having escaped after the ceremony but before the fish fry and the consummation, but he understood it to have been a good party. Nineteen years ago, he notes. Almost two decades.

"Thank you." Mirrors facing the elevator, brocade wallpaper, new carpeting under foot, directional sign indicating number 69 tucked at the end of a long corridor. He raps twice on the door of room 69. The door is opened by Constable Hegarty. "Good afternoon, sir."

"Good afternoon. I have a customer here, I believe," says Walt. The moment he enters the room, his attention is grasped in a vice-like grip by a woman of riveting beauty sitting at the *escritoire*. He knows she must be his client's lover, Professor Ursula Vere. She is smoking a Turkish Oval, long legs crossed, the slit skirt revealing delicious thighs. She inclines her beautiful head, levels her soft, kohl-rimmed brown eyes at him, and gives him the flick of a wink. Smiling back, he crinkles his eyes in what he hopes is a fetching way until he hears a distinct throat clearing annoyance.

"Um, um," Walt hears a cough. "Mr. Semchuk, I presume?" He snaps his attention to his client, Celeste Kinderman who is sitting erect in a Queen Anne chair by the pseudo fireplace. He recognizes her from sonorous Law Society newsletters and board of director photographs in the lobbies of both the Paunchmen's and the Fossil Fuel clubs where she was among the first wave of women to be permitted membership. Rumour had it that she was one step away from the presidency of The Law Society. She is holder of the Order of Candidia, second class, and a prime candidate on the short list for Chief Justice of Alberia.

Fearing she may start blabbing, he holds a finger up to his

pursed mouth in a 'hush down' gesture and stands, addressing himself to Staff Sergeant Boot. "My client has nothing to say. My advice to her is to remain silent. Is she under arrest?"

"Nope. Not yet. Search and seizure. D'you want to see the warrant?"

"Nope."

"Shouldn't we examine the warrant?" Celeste butts in. Semchuk ignores her, and perches on the arm of Professor Vere's chair.

"Who's the prosecutor on this case? Special Prosecutions?"

"No, sir. This is a Special Task Force. The Man is…" He points up to the ceiling. "…high up there."

Walt turns toward Ursula, examining her with fascination. All in all, Celeste is an admirable woman but not someone he would invite over to enjoy his mineral collection. In contrast, he can already imagine the magnificent Professor Vere waltzing around through his rooms, sipping a snifter of cognac and cooing over his rutilated quartz gems and sparkling Castillian argonite.

"Well, if you're finished with these people for the time being, Augi, we'll be leaving. I don't think I'll leave my client to your brand of friendly chat."

"Don't worry, Mr. Semchuk, we won't try to interrogate your client."

"The hell you won't. I know what happens to my clients in the enemy camp."

Hegarty nods. Celeste looks scandalized at this indiscreet, offhand, familiar manner of almost publicly airing her dirty linen. "Is there to be no private consultation at this stage with counsel? Isn't there a Charter of Rights, or something, Mr. Semchuk?"

"Never read it. I suppose you boys will be staying here

a while, examining your loot?" They nod. Walt dials room service, raising his voice into castrato. "Hello, this is Celeste Kinderman, in room 69. I'm famished for a light snack. Would you please send up chips, salsa, and a bottle of single malt make it Glenlivet." Then he adds, still impersonating his client, "Make sure to put it on my tab."

The Staff laughs. "Glad you're on this one, Mr. Semchuk."

"Oh, detail, I suppose you've frozen all her accounts," Walt asks the Staff, and Boot nods.

"Yes. We coordinated a seizure of all of Mrs. Kinderman's accounts," replies the Staff. "Bos Taurus, Montexia …umm… Ordland and Eurostein," he recites, adding, "don't take any cheques."

"Like that, is it," rejoins Walt. Boot and Hegarty are smiling. Ursula is making the odd note. Celeste now looks at the floor, her arrogance somewhat deflated. "Hey, by the way, do her law partners know?" This time, Boot and Hegarty shake their heads in unison.

Boot says, "Our instructions were strict, 'need-to-know', as they say. Warrants were executed on this room 69, the Posh Royal house, the Beesknees acreage, the lot. But law office records are always there, and we were …well, maybe I'll leave it at that, Mr. Semchuk."

"Well you obviously froze her Candidian bank records. That's like waving a red flag."

"Nope. Lemme just say…not our move. They were frozen by…another agency."

"Provincial."

"Might be, Mr. Semchuk."

"Yes. You boys keep this up, you may become efficient."

Celeste remembers she is a senior solicitor, and finds her voice again. "Shouldn't we examine all those warrants and things?" she demands.

"We?" repeats Walt. There is no mistaking his nuance, and Celeste slumps again. Walt rubs his eyes. *Why are all clients such assholes?* He draws a deep breath.

"Okay," he says, at last, "No problem with our interviewing a possible Crown witness, chaps?" indicating Ursula.

"No, sir. One thing, sir. We require to search your client before she departs this room. Do you consent on her behalf?"

"Go ahead," says Walt, making for the door but at the same time, the waiter arrives with the snacks and whiskey. He pours himself a whiskey and fans his hand over the food tray in an invitation for the others to have a snack.

Celeste springs to life, dips a chip, and pipes up. "Isn't there a constitutional safeguard against illegal search and seizure?"

"This one's legal," says Walt. "Consider your options. You can be arrested and searched and spend the night at the Crowbar Hotel, or you can be searched here and walk out with me. They'll give you a receipt. You know, if they take away your, er, dildos, or something."

Celeste and Ursula toss each other knowing glances then shrug and walk over to the table, dumping the contents of their purses on it, including, as Walt predicted, not only dildos but ribbons, feathers, and pink rubber hoses that may have been designed to tie back their hair, or for some other, more intimate purpose. "Help yourself," says Ursula, hoping that no one notices her favourite pair of fishnets poking out from the suede-lined secret compartment of her jewel bedazzled handbag.

Walt sees her handling the soft and sensual silk but does not let on and instead surveys the pile of titillating evidence, saying to the cops, "Well, gentlemen, I'll leave you to sort this out among yourselves." To Celeste he says, "I'll see you and your, er, wife at ten A.M. tomorrow, at my office. These gentlemen will not be listening." He hands her a calling card, hoping she has some ready cash. To Ursula he says. "Perhaps I might have a word with you over drinks in the Rooftop Lounge." He thinks about the tenderness with which she touched the beautiful, fragile stockings and then looks down at the evidence table and its array of toys, knowing that Ursula's interview is crucial to the case. He is also hoping that she swings both ways.

He departs, leaving the Glenlivet for the cops and steers Ursula toward the door.

UP IN A QUIET CORNER of the Rooftop Lounge at the Bos Taurus Dilettante Hotel, Walt Semchuk interviews Ursula Vere. The bar is done up as befits a business establishment in a moneyed city with delusions of grandeur — a sparkling wall of sapphire vodka bottles illuminated by throbbing track lights, crystal martini glasses bearing olives the size of walnuts, and a DJ spinning the latest in German *Sturm und Drang* house sounds remixed with Brazilian nouveau tango.

"You don't have to speak to me—" he begins.

"I know all that." She gives him a saucy look. "I want to help. I'll tell the same thing on the stand."

"Well, perhaps we can begin with what you know about all this?"

The server, who is gliding and swaying to the music like a cheetah in heat takes their order, giving Ursula time to refine and edit her disclosures about the Ordland debacle in which she finds herself swirling.

"Not much. Celeste is a secretive person. She had some hush-hush dealings with the government—"

"Federal?"

"No. Provincial. She did most of it out of room 69."

"How long?"

"I rented the room, oh, over a year and a half ago. I got number 69. We both liked *soixante-neuf*."

"I rather gathered that, Professor Vere."

"As a matter-of-fact," she adds, "when those police busted in, I was right in the middle of some … rather important business of an intimate nature. Put me off my stroke."

"I imagine it would," Walt responds, aroused and amused.

She takes a Turkish Oval from a tin cigarette box in her purse and Walt rushes to light it with her jewelled lighter. As he brushes by the tawny, honey-coloured skin of her extended hand, he is glad that smoking laws are changing back in favour of indoor smoking, at least at the best establishments.

"Don't see many of those," says Semchuk, observing the uniqueness of her Turkish Oval.

"Can't stand filters. Celeste picks these up for me in Istanbul." She looks at Walt, who makes a mental note. "She travels a lot. Anyway," she continues as she blows a sultry puff of smoke from her exquisite nostrils, "I've worked with Mrs. Kinderman as a participating associate at Burwash Kinderman for almost two years. I am also a professor at the law school and still have tenure up there but despite being a law prof, I know my way around cases like this." She pauses, sizing up his intellect. "I presume you want me to be frank?"

To this Walt nods a firm affirmative.

"About a year before I started working for her, as I understand it from our briefing sessions, she got a call from former Premier Ludwig and I know she attended a high-level meeting. The only record on the file is a memo of the date and place."

Anticipating a request from Walt, she says, "The police haven't hit her office at the firm yet for all the files. I checked."

"It's evidence, and has to be preserved and protected."

"So whose side are you on?"

"That's the law and the ethics of it. And that's my last word on it." He pauses, rather wishing he could bury his face in the soft folds of her neck. He continues, "I suspect that the investigators have all that they need, anyway, from down in room 69, and they can subpoena you. And you're not dumb—"

"That's kind of you, Mr. Semchuk."

"Not at all, Professor Vere. So you'll be a good witness for them. But it is rare and unusual that they wouldn't hit the firm at the same time as room 69, so they don't want any of this to get out, and they don't want any street rumours. Lawyers blab more than most."

"Mrs. Kinderman won't be blabbing."

"Damn right she won't."

"Just after I started working with her, Celeste told me to get a secure premises near the office, but unobtrusive, as she put it. So I leased the suite here at the Dilettante. Whatever she was doing for the government was conducted out of there, never at the office, not even phone calls. She would get calls there, so she must have had some prearrangement from the calling parties, especially the overseas ones. And it was the mailing address, too. Until she got paranoid at one point, and changed the mailing address to my apartment. There's a stack of stuff there, by the way."

"Preserve it. Overseas? What exactly was she doing for the government?"

Ursula stretches her lovely arms over her head, causing Walt's eyes to glaze over. "Who knows! Only Celeste. I pieced together certain things, but we had better things to do down in the room, just for a break from the usual, you know." She stops for a moment to gauge his reaction to this reference to their sexual encounters. He looks confused so she gives his thigh a gentle squeeze under the table — a move that cheers him up fast.

Ursula continues, "You'll have to get the details from Celeste, if she'll tell you. As I said, she's pretty close with things. I mostly used 69 to blow off steam at the end of a busy day. And you needn't give me that sort of look. As I said, I want to help Celeste. We have a good relationship. She's not the pompous bitch she appears to be."

"You could have fooled me. What did you conclude about what she was doing?"

"As near as I could figure out, it has to do with the Alberia Government buying a commodity from an Ordland company. For a lot of money, and I mean a pisspot full of money."

"Buying what?"

"Gold."

"Gold?"

"G-O-L-D."

"Ordland doesn't have any gold mines, last time I looked."

"Good for you, Mr. Semchuk. You'll be a lawyer yet. The Ordland company was a go-between."

"And the actual seller?"

"Well, no one is meant to know that. I saw back-to-back contracts; letters of instruction from time to time to Ordland solicitors and accountants; trust remittances for payment of Ordland invoices; that sort of thing."

"And the winner is—?"

"Veltland."

Suspending his surprise and curiousity about the Veltland

connection, Walt feels it only common courtesy to make one observation at the solemn recounting of the frustrated suite 69 girl-to-girl lick-fest: "*Delictus interruptus*, Professor Vere? That's abominable! Oh infamy, oh blot on honour and religion."

"Milton. Good." She recalls the pleasant, subtle orgasm she experienced when removing her silk and lace fishnet stocking from Celeste's head. "Not to worry, Mr. Semchuk, it was not a Paradise Lost."

"You are a superior woman," murmurs Walt, more to himself than to her, then he gets back to the matter of Veltland, having taken the time to let his subconscious mull over the logic of the conversation. "Was the Ordland company a front for dealing with Veltland gold producers? Let's back up here a bit. A secret government meeting with Celeste," he muses. "And a minute of that meeting devoid of detail. Just the fact of meeting and who was present, you say?"

"Yes. Some innermost old boys in solemn and clandestine assembly with your illustrious client. A blimp of windbags, for sure."

"And the government was not buying gold shares or certificates or futures, or the like, on a Securities Exchange?" he asks. " I mean, wasn't it just using the Ordland company as an agent to trade on the world markets?"

"Nope," responds Ursula, "the back-to-back contracts were for straight purchases of gold bullion."

"Back-to-back contracts, utilizing an Ordland company. What was it called?"

"Numbered company. Unobtrusive, anonymous."

"On reflection," he says, "it shows a certain flair, a damn-the-torpedoes attitude, does it not? And the Ordland company is a front for dealing with Veltland gold producers.

Of course. Why is the right wing Alberia provincial government surreptitiously buying large amounts of gold bullion over a period of years from a right wing country that the current Candidian left-wing federal coalition doesn't much care for?"

"I guess you'll have to ask Mrs. Kinderman," she responds.

"That I will, that I will." He stands, extending his hand to her as she rises from the chair opposite. They make their way through the crowded bar, now populated with gyrating couplings of trendies.

They ride the elevator down to the parking lot, in a turmoil of curiosity about each other now. They share an unspoken approval of their multiple selves in the fragmented smoky mirrors — a fun-house of pheromonic tall and sultry This causes a couple of riders, travelling from the spa level to the lobby, to gasp and swoon in the presence of their splendour. 'Power Couple' cannot begin to define the seductive energy and manipulative potential of Walt and Ursula.

Reaching the parking level, Walt composes himself and shakes off the urge to kiss her luxurious mouth. "Thank you, Professor Vere. You've been most helpful."

"You'll be calling me again, Mr. Semchuk."

"Most certainly."

"Then you'll need my number." She writes her private number on the back of her card.

They walk over to their vehicles, parked side by side and start the engines; his a heaving Ford F150 and hers a limber BMW 3 series coupé.

"Mr. Semchuk…What's your first name, anyway?"

Down rolls Walt's window. "Vladimir, but everyone calls me Walt."

"I shall call you Vlad and you may call me Professor Vere."

They rev their engines, laugh and jockey position for a sprint to the exit ramp and on into a moonlight ride through the glass-towered, amber-lit streets of Bos Taurus. At a red light along a curve of the Blow River, Walt shouts out to her, "I'll be in touch, Professor Vere," to which she answers, "I have no doubt of that, Vlad." She guns her engine and leaves him in the dust.

AT 10 O'CLOCK the next morning, right on cue, Ingrid intercoms. "Mr. Semchuk, the Kindermans are here."

"Okay. But let them wait a bit. As Francis Bacon said, it is good a little to keep state. I will simulate a grave mien, which is important when one is about to relieve a new prospective client of a great deal of boodle."

Walt decided long ago that the first interview with the client should always be brief. He knows enough about Celeste to figure that she would be back to her ridiculous pecker-headed self now that the shock of detection has worn off to some extent. She would be assertive of her supposed rights and position because her wife will be present. Walt therefore decides to give her short shrift, and to double charge her from the start.

As Mrs. and Mrs. Kinderman enter his office, Walt rises, making it appear to be a great effort and for the benefit of Celeste's wife.

"May I introduce my wife, Flossy Megadoll," says Celeste.

"Hello," says Walt, holding out his hand to Celeste's über-feminine lifemate, who looks back at him with a sunny smile. "Charmed," she giggles, and Walt feels compelled to kiss her cheek, an action that causes a reproachful stare from his client, the other Mrs. Kinderman. As her name suggests,

Flossy is not afraid of extreme makeup, hair extensions, and clothes that show off her curves. Today she is dressed in a summer outfit, a soft-pink low-cut *chinois* satin dress, a floppy violet sun hat and strappy sandals with four-inch platform soles that make her boing when she walks.

They sit down on the edges of their chairs. Walt tilts in his comfortable chair, crosses his legs, and puts his feet on the edge of his desk. "The first thing we'll discuss is the retainer."

"Well, that's no problem. You bill me monthly for your time, Mr. Semchuk, and I'll—"

"Do you have the title to your house?"

"What's that got to do with this?"

"Collateral, for my fees. Otherwise, up front, Mrs. Kinderman. One hundred percent down and nothing to pay."

"Look here, why do I have to post money like a common criminal—"

"Because certain people high up, as they say, in the province think you are a common criminal," rejoins Walt. Celeste shrinks, appalled.

"D'you own your own house?" Walt shoots at her.

She raises mournful eyes. Walt notes they look jaundiced, puffy, old.

"My wife does."

"Clear title?"

"Yes."

"Posh Royal, I suppose."

"Yes. And an acreage at Beesknees. It's joint property."

"All right, fifty thousand bucks up front, deposit the title to the house with an executed transfer in my favour."

"That is outrageous."

"Let's move on, shall we. You understand," he says to Flossy Megadoll, "that your wife is probably going to be charged with serious criminal offences." Flossy's smile melts. No doubt she is horror struck at the threat to her position in queer society and to her fashionista credit rating.

Flossy squeezes out a response. "I know nothing about these things but I'm sure my wife is quite innocent."

"If she is charged, it'll be in all the papers. I want to warn you of that, and on television and all over the place."

Celeste responds as Walt has predicted. "This is an outrage. If the press publish anything, I'll sue them. I instruct you to get an injunction."

"Mrs. Kinderman, publicity is the hallmark of a judicial enquiry," intones Walt with great satisfaction. "You know the press can report the fact of charges with total impunity."

"Semchuk, I came to you, umm, and of course Fred Fiddler, because they say you two are the best in your field."

"I am," agrees Walt, "Fred is getting there."

"It is an area of law with which I have neither experience nor expertise, of course."

"That is also true, I'm sure," Walt agrees again.

"Nevertheless, I must take issue with the rather casual manner in which my interests have so far been represented by you."

Walt gives her the cold stare he reserves for lying witnesses. He waits some dramatic moments. "You finished?" he enquires.

"I believe so. I want you to know from the outset that I have done nothing illegal and nothing of which I need to be ashamed."

"Quite," responds Walt.

The while, Flossy puts her hands on her face and sobs, dabbing her eyes so as not to smudge her extreme mascara.

"Flossy," says Walt, "would you be good enough to wait

for us in the reception area. I'm sure Ingrid will be happy to make you a martini."

She rises, throwing off a garden of fragrance. Walt finds himself wondering if she was born a woman or if she is transgender. "Mr. Semchuk," Flossy begs, "please do all you can to help my wife. She is a fine and good woman. I believe in her as do a great many people in our community. This is all a terrible blow to her. And for us. Please spare no effort in her defence."

And no money either, thinks Walt to himself. It is a brave little speech. Even Celeste looks like an orphan, lost in the wilderness. But only fleetingly. Walt stands up, and smiles at Flossy. "Worry not, my dear," he tells her, "I'm the best in the business. I'm not a modest man. I don't like to lose. Your wife is not on trial, I am." Flossy tips her head quizzically then boings out of the office.

Walt waits until the door closes after her then engages Celeste Kinderman QC, with vigour.

"Now Celeste, let's cut the crap. Two very experienced senior policemen — at least two — and some very experienced high-ranking prosecutors, think you are a crook. They intend to put you in jail. For a long time. Is that clear?"

"In jail?" That concept has not crossed Celeste mind. "That's unthinkable," she splutters, "unacceptable!"

Walt continues. "The only person who has an even chance of keeping you out of the jail, where you probably deserve to be, is me. So from now on you take my advice, which means you will do what I tell you to do and you'll keep your trap shut."

"I'm not used to being spoken to in this fashion."

"So get another lawyer. If you want, I'll give you the names of three good old boys of the criminal bar who will be happy to take all your dough and let you do and say what you want and fuck it up and kiss you off."

Celeste sits there looking down her nose at this person of lower orders, of low degree, this 'criminal lawyer'.

"I tell you something, girl. You're in trouble. The fuzz don't kick in the door of the average play room, nor do they freeze the bank accounts of the average player. Whatever you've done, and I'll hear your version in due course, it's a federal case. You're for the high jump."

Celeste sighs, and looks pained, as if she has a gas obstruction in her bowel. At length, she speaks. "I must defend myself with every means at my disposal."

Walt tilts his head to one side. There are a lot of missing pieces. He has one burning question of this snobbish woman across the desk, arising more out of curiosity than any relevance it might have to the instant proceedings. "Why has the Alberia government been buying up large amounts of gold bullion?" he queries.

"They didn't tell me and I didn't ask. But they are not going to prosecute anyway. Publicity for this secret enterprise is the last thing the provincial government wants. Nobody knows except a few very, very select people." She clams up.

Walt commands, "Name them."

She sighs and shifts her hefty hips in the squeaky chair reserved for nervous clients. Biting her lip, she says, "The former Premier Mad Ludwig — and he's dead."

"Well I suspect the former premier would have known about it. Who else?"

"A high-ranking civil servant —"

Walt jumps in, "And who would that be?"

Celeste hesitates, sitting back. The chair squeaks.

"I asked you," he presses. "Who would that be?"

She answers his question. "Baycell Sharpe."

"Sharpe. Hmmmm. The Deputy Attorney General?" He coughs. *So I'll be dealing with the notorious Sharpie,* Walt thinks to himself. He stands to usher Celeste from the room. "Well, that's enough for today."

"Good day, Mr. Semchuk." She brightens up and stands, looking at him over top of her reading glasses. "Who knows, Mr. Semchuk, there could be a huge pot of gold at the end of this rainbow. I...umm... have the fullest confidence in you."

"So do I, Mrs. Kinderman."

AFTER THIS CONVERSATION, Walt dials.

"Professor Vere? Walt Semchuk."

"I have been awaiting your call, Vlad."

"Perhaps a few oysters and champagne, Professor Vere, say eight-ish?"

"I would be delighted."

FOUR

'A FEW OYSTERS AND CHAMPAGNE' at the Dilettante Rooftop Salon ushers in the era of lust and revolution between Mr. Walter Semchuk and Professor Ursula Vere. In the elevator ride to the parking lot, Walt wordlessly moves toward her without a smile, without a sound, her mossy odor drawing him into a kiss that soars him past the smoky mirrors, out past the moon and the sun and on into a vast fluid constellation of stars. They fly through the night, arriving at Ursula's apartment and into her soft, silky bed for a sensorial whirl of harmonized desire. Her body matches his exquisitely and in this moment of breathless passion he cannot tell where his body ends and hers begins. She guides Walt inside to join her in his final journey out into the universe of pleasure. In his great moment of unstoppable, uncontrollable lust she calls out "Vlad, give it all to me. Like you never have before." And he drills into her, insanely horny, groaning, "Yessss, come with me. This is our revolu-u-u-u-ution."

He is in her thrall. He lounges in her arms, and gazes wide-eyed into what he believes is her deepest inner life. At this moment his passions are hers, forever and for always. She traces her red-tipped fingers along his body and she gives him a playful whip on his firm, gleaming ass. She winks at him, knowing there is something still missing in her complete pleasure. She reaches over to her shiny, bejewelled handbag, and sneaks a quick rub of her lacey fishnets between her thumb and forefinger — a fetish without which her elation would be incomplete. In time, she may share her obsession with him but for now, she tousles his curls and coos, "Vlad, darling, it is now time to talk about our revolution."

Walt settles back and a mock seriousness descends on the tranquil scene. He begins by voicing his ideals in a dry monotone. "Decades of Candidian governments begin with promise and deteriorate to bloat and bilge. Our only choice is to start a revolution to take Alberia out of confederation so we can," he snorts, "save the oilsands."

Ursula laughs, knowing he is only telling half the story. "My dear, we are not complete nihilistic sophomores, particularly in view of the pot of gold I now know you know. It's the gold which really informs our revolutionary deliberations, isn't it."

He stares at her, breathless with her brilliance. She takes a Turkish Oval out of her cigarette case and he bustles to light it for her.

Ursula continues, "We still want a revolution because that will give us power. But revolutions inevitably consume themselves so it's just as well we end up rich." She takes a deep drag on her cigarette, "The government controls the gold so we have to become the government. Then we can control the universe."

Ursula thrills to the idea of a conspiracy with Walt Semchuk to take over the government of Alberia and end up rich. She shakes her thick dark hair and laughs as she reaches down and turns on her mobile, calling up the Overture to Wagner's *Tannhauser* on her wireless sound system. "We need an anthem for our revolutionary party that will stir the very souls of the proles and peasants. Listen, Vlad." They listen for a few moments to this somber work, lips pursed in rapt attention. Not connecting with the emotion of this music but not wanting to hurt her feelings, Walt scrolls through her song list and finds something he thinks Alberians can use to foment their revolution — a vintage song by the Rolling Stones, *Under My Thumb*. He fractures the lyrics, jumping up to strut the length and breadth of Ursula's hardwood.

Under our thumbs, Candidia which once had us down
Under our thumbs, ain't going to push us around.

Ursula responds, flushing with pleasure and leaping off the bed to join him in his dance using a satin sheet first like a bullfighters cape and then winding it around her like a sarong. He has never seen a more strong and beautiful dancer. She shouts over his singing, reminding him, "Vlad, there are noble musical precedents for memorializing a community. Music thematisizes revolutionary rapture!" Walt scrolls down through her vintage hits and finds The Who and makes up some lyrics on the spot.

Lift up your eyes
To the Great Revolution
Lift up your hearts
To the Al-ber-ia sol-uu-tion.

"I love it! Dreadful, banal crap," Ursula shouts to Walt.

"Yeah, I cranked it out on a sausage machine," Walt yells back.

"Vlad, that's pretty good but I'm not going to let go of Wagner especially when teamed with *Tannhauser*. Wagner worked for Hitler, you know."

"Professor Vere, you may be right but if one does not understand the role of a banal sausage machine jingle, one does not understand domination." They roll and rock together to his new anthem *Lift up your Eyes,* taking turns fracturing the lyrics and he locks back into her seductive arms. They fall back across the satin sheets. He knows he has a ruthless partner in the revolution.

THE NEXT MORNING over Turkish Ovals, toast and marmalade, Walt and Ursula discuss their action plan for implementing an Alberia revolution.

Walt pours some coffee. "I've been an Alberia separatist probably all my life," he tells Ursula, "and my family before me, so money and power are strong motivators, but I must admit to have some sentimental devotion to Alberia and our superior way of life. To make this revolution work we need to study how it worked before: totalitarianism and the abuse of power."

Ursula is fascinated. "I share the same interests for the same reasons, darling — the gold, the oilsands, and the legacy of our superiority."

He spreads blood marmalade on his toast. "We're not testing theories here. We can take a democratic polity, say Alberians in their present frame of mine, and unite them to go whole hog to right-wing separatism."

"There are three conditions that will motivate Alberian citizens to be a mob," she says: "First, a charismatic leader; second, the current uncertain economic and political times; and third, there have to be identifiable groups that threaten the average Alberian." She thinks for a moment, "In Alberia, the mob turning points will be political and economic, namely those Eastern bastards and the environuts. Let's exploit those as the 'threatening factors', my dear Vlad."

He explodes with joy at her comprehension. "You've nailed it. Fred can be the charismatic leader, the attack on the oilsands is all about politics and the economy, and you've got it right about the hate groups."

She brandishes her Turkish Oval on high. "Witness the birth of the Alberia Special Party ... ASP!"

"ASP!" They both say and raise their crystal orange juice glasses, each to the other.

"ASP it shall be," Walt says. "I love it! How do we pull it off?"

"Well, remember Hitler was elected under similar conditions, it was not a *coup*. Alberians traditionally throw tired governments out, clean house, and start again with a new team. But the new team is invariably the same old crooks wearing different silly hats."

"That, my dear Professor Vere, will change under ASP... will change." He leans over to kiss her and raises his voice. "Under ASP we shall deliver a true alternative."

Ursula nods and contemplates the implications. "Then we will be in control. I favour the concept of the two of us as puppetmasters. And if I may be so bold as to remind you, we can put the ideological proselytizing and philosophical pretensions on hold for the moment, and keep our goals in mind: the oilsands and the gold. We take power, and we take them both."

He looks up at her and the morning sun catches his face. "Our joint revolutionary experiment encounters almost perfect conditions. The great majority of Alberians see 'those Eastern bastards' as a threat to their exploitation of their heritage, the oilsands. Alberia's biggest customer for oil, Montexia, stirred up by the environmentalists, is putting bans on the importation of 'dirty oil', while the Candidian feds are imposing draconian pollution controls. Another factor is that the provincial government is weak and irresolute and badly led, and is not seen to champion the wants and aspirations of the Alberian populace. People in Alberia are right-leaning in any event, and Fred Fiddler The Charismatic Leader steps into the spotlight at the right time—"

They both laugh, holding hands across the breakfast table.

Walt continues, "There has always been a strong undercurrent of separatism in Alberia, and with our friend JB Mailcoat and his seven seriously rich posse who covet the oilsands, there is the money to finance our revolution. We have only to tap into — that is, have Fred the Puppet tap into — the current moral malaise afflicting us."

"My dear Vlad, all of these factors coming together at the same time give you and me the opportunity and the impetus to set the wheels in motion."

She smiles and they go together over to her window. They put their arms around each other and watch the wide Blow River sweeping its way east. It is high this year with the big melt from the Blow Glacier. Walt is thoughtful and strives to impress her with his lofty cerebration. "I lament the era, Professor Vere. Overall, pervasive and lowering and levelling, it's the post-modern mannerist period of the sorry days, sloppy sentiment, socialism, and liberal democracy, and, for that matter, slipping standards, solipsism, and shit-eating."

"Don't get depressed by cerebral ideology, my dear Vlad. Let's keep our feet firmly on the earth, shall we? Think of Severus marching toward Rome. Be content with slinging a dead cat into the noon meeting of the Downtown Rotary Club."

Walt is cheered by her magnetic pragmatism. "You're right. It is the perfect time for Fred Fiddler to be in the full flight of his megalomaniacal ascent."

"Yes, partner-in-crime, the perfect time. The people want certainty and plenty and discipline and the strong forceful leadership of a charismatic *suzerain*…be he ever so risible."

Undermining his loyalty to his long-time law partner, the enthralled Walt says, "My dear Professor Vere, my law partner Fred has admirable unswerving devotion to his own self-aggrandizement, which he can realize in full flower as the new Cromwell." Ursula nods. Walt continues, "Fred is a walking personality disorder. He is a classic case of the narcissistic personality type — the admirable centre of his own artificial universe, which is his only reality. He claims infallibility of judgment. His views are defined by resentment, conspiracy theories, and hatred for 'lefties'. To our benefit, I am able to pipe into his delusions. Into Fiddler, I can program what we want."

Ursula cautions, "We must, however, and for our purposes, bear in mind Bertrand Russell's distinction: 'The megalomaniac differs from the narcissist by the fact that he wishes to be powerful rather than charming.' According to this description, Fred is more of a megalomaniac than a narcissist, which suits our purpose."

"As the poet said, 'We will shape and sharpen his purpose, point his passionate aim,' but he'll think he's doing it himself," resolves Walt.

"Do you think Fred understands all this?"

"No, of course not, Professor Vere, but we do. Just keep Fred out front, selling the revolution with his personal mission to rid Alberia of the leftist vermin and protect the folks from the 'obscene' Eastern coalition who plot with the enviros to steal or shut down our oilsands birthright."

Walt steps back from Ursula and flashes the stiff-arm salute. "*Heil* Fiddler!"

"Has a great ring to it," laughs Professor Vere.

Imagining the revolution has made Walt lusty. "There is so much to do, so little time in which to do it." He adds teasingly… "but other appetites have also to be fed. Let us take a break in our deliberations, Professor Vere." Just as he reaches for her curvaceous ass and she parts her willing lips, his mobile jangles the urgent ring that he cannot ignore. Walt answers and then whispers to Ursula that he has to take the call that Ingrid, his assistant, is patching through. It is from Baycell Sharpe, the Deputy Attorney General of Alberia. Ursula doesn't mind because it gives her a chance to extract a brand new package of black Chinese silk filigree stockings from under her pillow — ones that she has been waiting for just the right moment to open. Despite his lusty passion, Walt doesn't mind because he knows Baycell will get him closer to the gold.

"Mr. Semchuk," says the voice over the phone. "Baycell Sharpe. I understand you're acting for Celeste Kinderman."

"I am."

"We need to meet immediately. Two o'clock, your office."

"Is my client to be present?"

Walt's conversation is giving Ursula the chance to tie his free hand onto the bedpost with the new black stocking. She pulls up his shirt and blows kisses all over his firm belly. He kicks his legs and grimaces to keep from laughing as he responds to Baycell's intriguing proposition.

"No, just her counsel. And Mr. Semchuk, I cannot over-emphasize the importance of discretion in this matter. No doubt your client has told you what we're playing with here.

No doubt you find it very intriguing. Keep your mouth shut about this. There's much at stake here, politically as well as otherwise."

Ursula tips Walt back onto the mattress. In spite of this, Walt says, "Well, the politics are your problem, the otherwise may be my client's. You'd better be doing a good security job. Street rumours get out."

"So far, Mr. Semchuk, no one has any inkling of the real facts."

"Well, you brought the cops in on it. So much for secrecy."

"A specialist team, handpicked, of a local police force," rejoins Baycell, "seconded to and reporting only to me, working with discreet private investigators who've been on Mrs. Kinderman's tail for over a year."

Ursula continues to arouse Walt with her flicking tongue, working her way down his bare leg where she lingers long enough to loop his ankle through the carefully knotted silk of the other stocking.

Walt stifles his laughter and responds to Baycell saying, "Well, it won't be long before the whole world knows Mrs. K is in some sort of glue. She's what they call high profile."

"All the better that we deal with this thing forthwith, before it gets out of hand."

Walt struggles a little as Ursula ties his leg to the bed-frame. "Maybe my client should hold a press conference."

"That would be very unwise," says Baycell. "Two o'clock today," he says, and rings off.

"Vlad," Ursula murmurs as she straddles him and tightens his restraints. "Before you tell me about this man you call Baycell, we have some important business, you and me."

At two p.m., Walt sits at his desk as Baycell Sharpe, the Deputy Attorney General of Alberia, is ushered in by Ingrid. Sharpe glides into Walt's office like a hungry shark searching for a meal. He presents as portly but neat, not sloppy. He is attired in a sober civil service uniform: a black wool-worsted three-piece suit with a one-colour dark tie. This non-flamboyance, he wears year round. He has thinning hair over a bald pate and thick black-rimmed glasses. His overall expression is stern. They shake hands.

"There need be no preliminaries," says Baycell, straight off. "This meeting is without prejudice."

Walt rubs the painful stocking burns on his wrists. "Our conversation is privileged, between counsel. Everything stays at this table. Agreed?"

Baycell nods and says, "This is the story in a nutshell. The late Premier decided to buy gold with Heritage Trust Fund monies because he thought the bottom was falling out of the economy and wanted to preserve the fund. The gold was stashed in the Arsehold bunker at the old air base north of here. The premier was secretive and the only people who knew about it were me, as the senior civil servant, and the chairman of the Heritage Fund. The purchases were all accounted for in the annual fund statements under 'diversified investments'. Mrs. Kinderman, your client, was retained to purchase the gold discreetly for the government."

"How did she go about it and why is she facing charges?"

"She set up an offshore company in Ordland to do this discreetly. Her Ordland company bought gold from a Veltland supplier and sold the gold to Alberia. It was shipped directly to the Arsehold bunker from Veltland. She did this over a period of years."

Walt raises his eyebrows "Over years? How much gold

are we talking about?"

"Probably about a billion dollars' worth, give or take the odd million at today's prices."

Walt lets out a low whistle.

Baycell goes on, "We found out she was marking up the price."

"What do you mean 'marking it up'?

"It's this simple, Mr. Semchuk. We supplied her with the funds. The Veltland supplier sold the gold to her Ordland company for 'x' dollars an ounce. Her Ordland company sold the same gold to us for 'x' plus 'y' dollars an ounce. 'Y' dollars went to her secret account in Eurostein. Your client is a common thief."

Walt leans back in his chair and whistles, adding, "I take it Kinderman was pocketing a whack of cash per contract for herself. And that's what this is all about. How did you find out?"

Baycell says, "Incompetence on the part of her Ordland accountant who sent our filing department the Veltland contract by mistake. This was immediately reported to me."

"Well," says Walt, "Is she going to be charged? It's your move. I get the feeling all you want is your money back. You can't be anxious that this becomes public knowledge."

Baycell sits back and composes his urbane features. "Your client won't be charged." His fingers come together. "Let's cut to the chase. Yes, we want the differential. There is no hurry, these things take time."

Walt says, "Very well. I will secure our client's undertaking to hold her secret fund for the government." He walks over to the side cabinet, pleased with his wording, and pours each of them a drink. His wrists burn again, reminding him of Ursula and that they could be running the government soon. He can't wait to tell her that they are one major step closer to the gold. He sits down and puts it to Baycell, "Who knows about the gold stashed in Arsehold?"

"Just you, me, and your client."

Walt sips his whiskey. "What about the cops who did your investigation — Boot and Hegarty?"

"They don't know the story. They followed my orders. I handled the investigation myself."

Walt says, "That leaves the chairman of the Alberia Heritage Trust Fund and the guys who unloaded the payload."

"Former Trust Fund chairman, advanced dementia. No memory of it at all. The functionaries who unloaded it are..." Baycell stares hard at Walt, "...deceased." He smiles the smile of a shark. "I think you agree that we could both profit by this exclusive knowledge, Mr. Semchuk?"

"Partners, Mr. Sharpe?"

Baycell raises his glass. "Your health. Partners."

Revolutions always attract the
wrong sorts of people.

— Alan Bennett, *Diary*

PART TWO

ASP-irations

FIVE

RURAL ALBERIA is the initial target area for Fred Fiddler to lay his traps and bait and spew his banana oil. The venue for the founding rally of the Alberia Special Party is the large indoor hockey and rodeo arena-cum-community hall at Sunken Coulee, a farming and oil well community an hour away from Bos Taurus. It's a hot, dry afternoon in Indian summer. Massive coolers of specially labelled beer featuring the ASP snake symbol are stationed at the entrance doors for the two thousand prospective separatists who have lined up to hear Fred Fiddler, the dynamic leader who has just burst upon the political scene. From the moment the doors open to the folks anxious to get in, the popular Western band Alberia Slickers has been belting out crowd favourites, and they continue non-stop. There is a holiday atmosphere, tinged with anticipation of something new and exciting. Walt senses there is revolution in the air. Some happy souls are line-dancing at the back of the hall to *Water Can't Quench the Fires of Love*. The arena still reeks of bull shit from last week's 4-H exposition abetted by the pungent vapours from the groaning trays of free corndogs and hotdogs. There's cotton candy for the kids.

In the dressing room area used by the local hockey and curling teams sits the core action cadre of the ASP Inner

Circle. The cynical hosts Walt and Ursula sit with the money-men, JB and his seriously rich magnificent seven oil barons. In attendance, on orders from JB, are Slick the omnipresent bird dog, Dr. Mavis Wong, head of the ES team, and Harold Spincter, his EA.

Ursula has also invited her law firm associate and occasional lover, Celeste Kinderman QC. She tells Walt that Celeste is "a bright light, influential, connected, and should be 'of counsel' to the Party." Walt agrees with everything Ursula suggests. He also wants to keep an eye on Celeste because she is privy to the secret stash of gold.

The Inner Circle's uniform, crafted by the ad agency Botchi and Botchi, symbolizes the ASP theme. They all wear wide-brimmed, black, beaver-felt cowboy hats surmounted by prominent, sparkling ASP snake badges; red and silver neckerchiefs; black Western-cut shirts with pearl snaps; black boot-cut designer denims; and black highly polished cowboy boots. Ursula has worn her fetish fishnets for good luck under her denims and hopes to position herself in the front row between Walt and Celeste for stereoscopic leg rubs. For her part, Mavis is amused that JB's denims have perma-creases and is pleased that he has taken a corset to his beer belly.

Walt, knowing that florid language is a huge turn-on for Ursula, shares this characterization of the crowd with the others in the back room: "This lot is our quintessential constituency. A rabble of mostly far right-of-centre folks inhabit this clime. We chose this locus with care."

Says Ursula, "Indeed, Vlad, we have here a collection of laboratory specimens that would be hard to replicate in the larger urban centres." JB and his entourage do not completely comprehend the elaborate vocabulary nor do they recognize themselves in the Vere and Semchuk satire, but overall they agree that Sunken Coulee is their target market.

The citizenry peculiar to Sunken Coulee, longing in uncertain times for certainty and afflicted with nostalgia for the absolute, have now been crowding into the arena and community centre for well over an hour. The place is alive with music and free goodies. There has been a rush and a pushing, and shoving, fisticuffs, and bad medicine over the coveted front row seats, and the hired security goons have had a rough time dissuading the usual ruffians from occupying the special reserved section earmarked as such, the two front ranks at the far right of the seating facing the main stage. There is a wide centre aisle separating two rows of tin chairs and by now it is standing room only.

The main hall is swollen to the rafters and stressed at the outer limits. Walt and Ursula have divined the population demographic correctly in assessing the support for their radical revolution. Walt's instruction to Botchi and Botchi, as well as to the ASP volunteer rally organizers, has been blunt: "Beat the bushes, alert the media, and pack this place. We don't want an empty hall and an audience of one lost child and a parolee who wandered in by mistake." At the rally Ursula says, "Vlad, don't fash yourself about the quantum of attendees. They're all here, the ASP ideal of marginalized constituents." She identifies these constituents as "restless rustics, unemployed hands, and laid-off rig workers, yokels, neo-Nazis, gun nuts, pro-lifers, evangelists, lunatics, homophobes, homicidals, racists, and bingo players."

Mavis offers her opinion: "Right, Professor Vere, but let me add that the people who make up the majority of the Alberia voting population are ordinary folks. Moms and dads, working stiffs, professionals, storekeepers, farmers and ranchers, small businessmen and businesswomen. Single moms, all people with families and critical finances and mortgages, you know, the grassroots." Mavis is grateful for having been able to voice what she wanted to say but she is still a newcomer to party events.

Ursula looks skeptical, always in her superior mode, but she is gracious: "I am respectful of your views, Dr. Wong."

Walt nods to Mavis. "The marginalized that Professor Vere has identified are the ones we recruit to do ASP's necessary dirty work. The people you identify are the voters with the clout to put us over the top. They will be co-opted in time. We need them all."

"Yeah Bu'ub," echoes JB, "and if y'all need more dollars to git 'em all, just holler." Hollering is what one has to do, even in the backrooms, over the din from the celebratory crowd and the sound of the Alberia Slickers.

Fred is backstage in a private dressing room improvised from the manager's office. He is delivering his speech to the mirror for the tenth time, choreographing his bogus facial expressions and coordinating his absurd arm and hand gestures. He is attired in his high-feast-day black silk suit with built-up shoulders and the narrowed waist to show off his physique, which is still comely. A striking red-and-silver silk kerchief erupts from his jacket breast pocket, matched by the dyed red-and-silver carnation in his lapel.

By six-thirty P.M. the hall is agog and noisy with anticipation and speculation. The Sunken Coulee rally is a linchpin to the organizers. It has been preceded by a month of intense media blitz, signboards displaying Fred's handsome visage, and adroit blurbs advertising the emerging Alberia Special Party. The stage is bedecked with huge red-and-silver banners stretching around three sides, wings and back panel, floor to ceiling; the walls all about the periphery of the hall are festooned with the banners. They alternate with blowups of Fred Fiddler posters. In each pose, he thrusts only his noble head and shoulders at the viewer. In each, he wears the same black silk suit. He shows variations of pose and expression from poster to poster, each one of five variants showing off Fred's crafted "my God, war at any moment!" expressions that so amuse JB.

There is no stage furniture. Two huge video screens are mounted high up to the right and left over the stage to project a giant Fred to the far reaches of the hall. The Alberia Slickers have vacated the substage and to the amazement of the attending, adoring public, and the amusement of JB and his entourage, no less than sixty professional musicians of the Bos Taurus Philharmonic, hired and bussed in at considerable expense, are tuning up their instruments to the stern overview of the concertmaster.

Suddenly the stage is illuminated with powerful arcs of light and red and silver pyrotechnics. Tyler Rourke, a high-end local hero in an ASP uniform sprints to centre stage. The crowd loves Tyler, he's one of theirs: an Olympian silver medalist in snowboarding. This very presentable teenage lad throws his arms up in a victory salute and bawls into the microphone: "Hey everyone, good to see ya, the show is about to start!"Mrs. Peabody turns to the people behind her. "That's our Tyler, he sung in the church choir you know."

Tyler yells over the noise of the adoring crowd, "Hey folks, hey ladies and gentlemen." When he realizes he can't calm them this way he throws his arms back up in the air, lowering them like a gentle wave. The din subsides, then dies down to absolute silence. Now the conductor rises and raises his baton. On the downbeat, the orchestra swings into a stirring marching medley of popular songs.

A clump of heavy boots, and from the rear of the hall, down the centre aisle, marching two by two, are a drilled phalanx of men and women of the West, all attired in the ASP uniform with the calculated addition of black military belts adorned with blazing ASP belt buckles. They are bearing aloft eight-foot banners in the ASP colours alternating with Roman-style staves lofting high ASP letters and snake badges. The letters ASP are surrounded by gilt leaf, the carefully selected ASP snake badge glowing red on a silver background.

"We're on our way," Walt whispers to Ursula as they, the privileged persons of the Inner Circle and a dog named Slick follow the marchers down the aisle. The Inner Circle themselves are a sight to behold, symbolizing as they do the four portals of desirable, attainable Western superiority: Property, Position, Patronage, Power. They take to their reserved seats in the two front rows to the right of centre stage and Ursula settles in between Walt and Celeste.

ASP wants to put on a show of adherents, but is still in its recruiting infancy. Most of the marchers are unemployed local actors hired, drilled, and well paid for the occasion. There are also some purported recruits to swell the ranks, rounded up at the men's drop-in centre, cleaned up, dressed in steel-toed cowboy boots and ASP belt buckles, and handed a few bucks and the promise of a continuing meal ticket. "Oohs" and "ahhs" arise from the goggling audience, impressed by the contrived Hollywood glamour.

The voluminous orchestra, heavy on the brass and percussion, continues to blare pop themes as the marchers disperse to right and left but remain standing, lofting their flags, banners, and badges throughout the entire show. At the same time, from both wings, two groups of large men and big women in red-and-silver hardhats and full swamping gear with steel-toed gumboots and heel clicks emerge single file across the rear of the stage and meet in the middle and turn to face the audience. The Oilsands Miners Chorus takes its place in history. The music ends. Silence. Bated breath, in the packed hall. The chorus leader, a big-shouldered female miner, possibly a cousin of Brunhilde, steps away from the chorus line and struts downstage, facing the singers. She turns and looks at the conductor. The conductor lifts his baton, nods, and the orchestra and the Oilsands Miners Chorus erupt into the opening bars of the "Independent Alberia Anthem."

> *"Lift up your eyes*
> *To-oo the Great Revolution*
> *Lift up your hearts*
> *To the Al-ber-iah sol-uu-tion."*

From the front row, JB yells to Walt, "Sure stirs them buggers up some." And the orchestra brings the piece to a close with crashing chords.

"Jeeze!" from an impressed JB, as the crowd rises as one quivering, blubbering mass, with wild cheers and sustained euphoric applause.

"The standard Bos Taurus knee-jerk standing ovation," Celeste whispers to Ursula as she moves her fingers up Ursula's inner thigh. "Darling," Ursula whispers back, "the crowd is moved." Walt notes their interaction with some irritation.

The entire audience remains standing in anticipation and there is an eerie collective consciousness. Ursula removes Celeste's fingers from her thigh, takes Walt's hand and says, "It's working so well, it's almost as if they have been pre-programmed." The adulatory din retreats, then dies again to silence. And still they stand. The main event is on its way.

Back in the second row, Mavis whispers to Harold, "This is bizarre! In Alberia!!??" Harold pretends not to hear. Mavis, disappointed with Harold's diffidence, mumbles to herself *what am I doing here? I need a stiff drink and a smoke.*

Fred Fiddler strides in, exuding confidence and control, and takes his imposing stance centre stage front, in a blinding spotlight. He has no notes. Sustained applause. There is no "Mr. Chairman" this, no "Ladies and Gentlemen" that, no "Friends, Romans, Countrymen", no preamble whatsoever. He launches at once into his scripted diatribe, delivered as if off the top of his handsome head. Fred is a natural rhetoric monger, a spellbinding orator, a mesmerizer.

Silence in the hall.

"You, the citizens of this, the most advanced and productive province in Candidia, have decreed enough is enough. You, the citizens, have had a bellyful, have had it up to here," he gestures his hands to his forehead, "with those Eastern bastards." The crowd cheers. "Those predatory Eastern bastards, those two-faced Eastern bastards! Shutting the oilsands down!" The crowd roars approval.

"No way! I say to you now, as one of you, Alberia born and bred, our time has come!" Along with his calculated pause there are scattered yells. "We're taking Alberia out!" Wild cheering emerges from the crowd along with foot stomping, clapping, folks patting strangers on the back, handshaking, thumbs up.

Fred's voice drops a crafted tone, for effect, for gravity. "Ask yourself, why are the feds and the enviros moaning and groaning over dead ducks when our jobs and livelihood are being wiped out? Why are we getting the end of the stick with the coat of Eastern excrement?" Catcalls and yelling come from the crowd. Fred continues with a crib from JB: "What kind of a lunatic political system tolerates a cobbled-together conspiracy that is trying to shut down our oilsands? Coalition? It's a calculated conspiracy!" Cheers, more foot stomping, people nodding their heads up and down, exchanging *we thought so* looks, "...a coup conceived in conspiracy and shame more sinister than anything manufactured by a banana republic cardboard Generalissimo..." Now stooges in the crowd let out rebel yells and whoops, which are taken up by prospective candidates for the Fiddler Youth.

Walt shouts to JB, sitting beside him in the front: "The Alberia Rebel Yell will be a big item, mark my words."

"Rebel-wha?"

"Do not tax yourself, Mr. Millcott."

"Mailcoat."

"Yes, I know that."

"... to cheat the electorate and topple from legitimate power a lawfully elected government!" Cries of "Shame!" and "Hang the bastards!" from the crowd. "What free and democratic country...? What free and democratic country...? Would allow a degenerative slime of lefties and Communists —" loud angry murmurings, rebel yells "—to cobble a conspiracy to shut down our oilsands, and perpetrate a fraud upon all the citizens of a once-proud country!"

Cobble a conspiracy. I like that. Walt smiles.

"I say to you, I say to all of you, no more. No more! No more will our fair province.... We own our resources, but they are trying to shut them down, right under our noses." Boos and jeers. "We must be vigilant! They want to prevent us marketing our birthright, our birthright, our fabulous rich oilsands, the second largest reserve of petroleum in the world! They want to shut them down, all over a few dead ducks. They, those Easter scum, want to strip us of our wealth and even stop us from pipelining our life-enhancing product to our friends in Montexia and the FarEast."

Fred reaches his zenith. "Enough, citizens of Alberia. Enough of snivelling, sniggering, swaggering office-holders, securing their sinecures at the sordid trough of swinish patronage!"

Walt has to suppress a yelp of laughter and to hold his sides as he shakes with enjoyment. He turns to Ursula. "This is going better than our most extravagant predictions." She says, "I've had enough of Fred, I need a break."

She pulls out her case of Turkish Ovals and feels a tap on her shoulder. She turns. Mavis, in the second row, points to the cigarettes with a questioning look. Ursula nods and they escape to the side exit. JB admires Mavis for holding her own with that pushy broad, Ursula Vere. He approves of the tilt of her cowboy hat and thinks maybe she put on some lipstick.

As Fred Fiddler rants on with his trademark brand of insubstantial oratory, a hollow harangue by any cursory analysis, Mavis and Ursula find a pleasing rapport in sharing a smoke break.

Mavis says, "I guess I shouldn't say this, thinking of my job and all, but this is kind of frightening, don't you think?"

Ursula looks coolly at Mavis, sizing her up and expelling smoke through her nostrils. She says, "It's the times, my dear. Might as well be in on the ground floor, otherwise your face will be pressed against the glass from the outside." She produces a small flask of cognac, takes a slug and offers it to Mavis.

Mavis swallows the fiery fluid, and says, "You and Walt started all this, didn't you? You sucked JB into this, didn't you?"

"You have it wrong. JB brought us into this. It was because of the dying ducks. You should know better than anyone that he has to make this duck mess go away. I heard that you are the one who found the ducks so it's all because of you really, not me."

"Oh shit. I never thought..." She stops and shakes her head. "That's unacceptable. I don't have to take that, I was just doing my job."

Ursula says, "The fact is, there are outside forces trying to shut down the oilsands because of all the dead ducks. That's why those people are here."

"What's that supposed to mean? I did my time in Tapperlite and we came to grips with environmental problems. We didn't duck them. I think I can make a difference with Mr. Mailcoat's company."

"Well, don't hold your breath, my dear." She looks at Mavis. "But I think you and I are going to get along."

"Well, maybe—"

At that moment, Tyler Rourke comes around the corner, enjoying a toke. They give him a nod and Ursula says, "You did great, kid. Hope you'll join the party. We have a youth wing planned." And then to Mavis, "Let's go back in, I'm sure we haven't missed a thing." Walking back, Ursula enjoys the whisking silk of her stocking between her inner thighs.

Mavis checks her mobile and sees a tweet coming in on the DuckinOil hashtag. *I heard someone made a sticker with PetroFubar's logo and a picture of a duck. It said 'PetroFubar doesn't give a duck.'* The response is, *I also heard the person got fired. Does anyone know if this is true and if so where I could buy this sticker?*

BACK IN THE ARENA, Fred is dwelling in his *dénouement* upon the unlawful criminal strictures placed upon the Alberia oilsands resources; the punitive emissions standards making oilsands development almost impossible; the pending hated carbon tax; and the straight unchecked and unpunished larceny of the federally pumped up equalization payments. Fred scowls and points his square finger, "Equalization payments? Are we to be forever bamboozled by Orwellian doublespeak? How about un-equalization payments?" Whether or not the crowd really understands anything more than the words 'bamboozled' and 'doublespeak,' they still politely clap their approval.

At this point, a dissenter in the crowd at the back of the hall shakes his fist and cries "Shame on you, shame on all of you!" Ursula, now back in her seat after her smoke break, scoffs to Walt "The usual scruffy lout trying to make a statement." A couple of other poor youngsters wave crudely lettered signs: *Fascist! Nazi!* Fred pauses, with telling effect. "Oh, I see we have some Eastern sympathizers, some nancy boys here!" The pathetic lads are at once set upon by rough elements in the crowd, beaten, and expelled with extreme prejudice, to enthusiastic encouragement from the older folks.

Now Fred stretches himself to his full six-foot-two plus, with the assistance of elevator shoes, to deliver his grand slam.

"Citizens of Alberia, will you join me in this revolution, our revolution, for it is nothing short of a revolution!" The crowd, stirred up by the violence against the peaceniks, cries out *yes, yeah, and Aww-ri-i-ite.* "And make no mistake," continues Fred. "We are in for a battle, we are in for the fight of our lives. Join with me in this glorious enterprise, citizens, and you shall be my brothers and sisters!"

The Oilsands Miners Chorus bursts into a last song, planted by JB as his contribution to sell Fred to this crowd,

Oh give me sands lots of sands 'neath the starry skies above
Don't close 'em down
Let the oil ooze and run through the pipelines that I love
Don't close 'em down.

The song moves the crowd to even more extravagant hoorahs. "Damn rights, worked like stink," says JB to no-one in particular. Fred turns dramatically, and strides off the stage. The place goes crazy. Cries of "More, more!" reverberate through the hall. The orchestra, taking its cue, plunges into a crashing *finalé*. People mill about and are enthused, energized, illuminated, and above all, Walt notes with satisfaction, politicized.

Fred Fiddler does not reappear. Walt has admonished him never to make a curtain call, never to provide an encore, no matter what the clamour. Always leave the great unwashed wanting more. The legend will grow exponentially.

The orchestra flourishes the end of its piece. People mill and visit happily, loathe to leave.

WALT CONVENES an impromptu post-mortem. Fred is puffed up with his own glory, pumped up by his own puissance, transported by his unbridled vanity. Walt throws Fred a bone and, in turn, lets JB gnaw on it for his share of the glory: "I like the old Bing Crosby crib, Fred. Just the perfect call for this lot."

"Yes."Fred examines his noble face in the hand mirror he carries in his pocket. Walt gestures for the undivided attention of JB and his sordid oilpatch henchmen and fellow sponsors of ASP, the seriously rich magnificent seven. Some of them have already been promised cabinet posts once ASP forms a government.

Harold pours single malts. The assemblage, flushed with its first overwhelming success, drinks a toast to Fred. Fred preens, like the bride at a country wedding. Celeste networks the Inner Circle, handing out her card. Mavis alone has reservations but she remains in the room, in loyalty to JB.

Walt holds up his hand. He speaks. "The Independent Alberia Anthem vouchsafes the people a sense of shared achievement, a sense of shared belonging, a sense of shared accomplishment, a sense of shared ambition carried to the heights."

Ursula then adds, "It is at once the rallying musical cry for our revolutionary forces. It symbolizes the outreach of ASP through early adversity to political domination." She sees Mavis rolling her eyes back. Mavis thinks *that ASP song is a musical Pepto-Bismol. It coats everything including the vomit.*

The Oilsands Miners Chorus members have already been politicized by their chorus leader, one Hannah Stroud, of Teutonic ancestry. Walt has invited Stroud to join the Inner Circle on this auspicious occasion. She volunteers the *raison d'être* of the Chorus. "We ain't no pansy-ass cupcakes! Them sortsa arseholes don't survive in this gal's oilsands!"

JB, thinking from her drawl that she is a fellow Montexian yells in approval, "Fuckin' A."

Applause from The Inner Circle. "Bravo," rejoins Ursula, amused by such overt bumpkinry. Hannah excuses herself to "join the boys at th' bar, we got some celebratin' of our own to do. Wanna join us, JB?" To which he says, "I'll catch ya later." She goes on, "We're loyal to th' ASP cause, Leader. Count on us." She flashes Fred a stiff-arm salute. Fred returns the salute, his jaw set in what he considers the Napoleonic mode.

"What a gaggle of hard-hatted morons," Ursula sneers to Walt, in a whisper.

They disperse, wearied but high in oath. JB takes the occasion to sidle up to Walt. "Hey, ya know somethin', they like this Fred Fiddler guy!"

Says Walt, "He has, as they say, the common touch." Thinks Walt, *this is going to be even easier than I thought.*

SIX

L AST WEEK'S SUNKEN COULEE RALLY has made one fact plain. In matters requiring judgment, Fred is dependent upon the advice, counsel and direction of Walt and Ursula. He is lost without them.

It is the night before a scheduled meeting with the Inner Circle to finalize the ASP party's platform and Walt and Ursula are drinking black beer and eating shelled peanuts at Clobbers, an after-hours upscale boozecan in downtown Bos Taurus. They started the evening out in much more sophisticated surroundings at the Fizzique Club but Flossy Megadoll spotted them from the stage during her midnight show and hissed her song "Honey Suck My Rose" at Ursula in a territorial display of venomous jealousy. Seems Celeste must have admitted the affair.

Clobbers has cleared out, save for a fat fellow in the corner wearing a cheap straw cowboy hat with a blowsy woman on his lap drinking potato champagne. She is puling on and off in a loud rasping voice about her sex-maniac manager at the supermarket who is always trying to cop a feel on the job. This puts Ursula in a frame of mind to discuss her favourite maniac, Fred.

Walt reaches over and pops a peanut into Ursula's mouth. "Vlad," she says between chews, "I was impressed by Fred's performance in front of the Sunken Coulee crowd. You were right about his charm. His rhetoric was magnificent."

"Well, Professor Vere, Fred is the perfect blueprint for megalomania." Ursula leans over the table and licks the beer foam from the corners of his mouth. Walt continues, "He's so hungry, he's so thirsty, for power — political power, absolute political power— 'I, Caesar! I, the Sun King!' — he'd sell his own granny into slavery if it got him one inch nearer. He would take the gold out of her back teeth!" He adds, "Fred isn't big on social justice."

"Fred's idea of social justice would be killing communist women and children."

"Quite, Professor Vere. I've seen it. Fred Fiddler is one scary guy, but a one-dimensional scary guy. He yearns for public office, any public office, provided it is high office. Offer him a carrot … let's just say he's easily manipulated."

"So let's give him his carrot." She flourishes the cocktail napkin from under her beer glass. "Better still, let's give him a bunch of carrots." She takes out a pen and unfolds the napkin to its maximum dimension. "Okay, Vlad, I know you've been thinking about this for years."

Walt runs through the details in his mind to be sure his mental list is in order. "Fred and the Inner Circle have to accept that the true path to power is in telling lies, big lies. Really Big Lies to be hammered home with incendiary speechifying at every opportunity, in every venue."

"I was thinking the same thing. If you tell a big enough lie people will believe there is truth to it. Stalin and Hitler understood this."

Then and there they concoct the party platform. The contents of the cocktail napkin sets the stage for the revolution and dictates the terms for all future dealings with Fred

Fiddler by the founders of the revolution.

Ursula says, "Understanding, Vlad, that the revolution is bogus. It's just the smoke and mirrors we sell to the folks out there. The revolution to them is independence, shaking off the old chains, that sort of nonsense. The revolution to us is something more basic: we take the government, we take Alberia out, we own the oilsands, you and I get the Arsehold Gold." As if to add an exclamation point to this conversation, the blowsy woman lets rip a tremendous fart and falls off her companion's lap into the mounds of peanut shells on the floor.

THE NEXT DAY, heady with the success of the Sunken Coulee rally, JB holds court at the power brokers' Tycoon Room of the Fossil Fuel Club, with the express purpose of finalizing the ASP party platform. Fred Fiddler, Harold Spincter, an ebullient Celeste Kinderman, and JB's Inner Circle are already "tyin' on th' old feedbag" as JB puts it. JB has gifted each member of the Inner Circle with a hand-whittled duck decoy. The decoys float on the tables beside the bread and butter dishes like a froth of misguided wildlife. The male mallard he made for Mavis floats sadly beside her unused dining service. She has been, as she put it on the phone, unfortunately delayed.

Walt also declined breaking bread with "that gaggle of scumbags," as he describes them to Fred, but has informed Fred that "Professor Vere and I will attend the ensuing business meeting." Instead of putting up with the company of the Inner Circle, Walt and Ursula are at Walt's lavish downtown apartment listening to Bach and shaving each other's heads. Ursula has gone under the needle for a coiled asp snake and dripping blood tattoos that now cover her arms and shoulders and is wearing black rubber-tight biker leathers, stilettos and her best seamed filigree leggings with a red lace corset. Walt has opted for a black slender-cut suit in the style of European soccer coaches, guys who, as he says, "know how to turn testosterone into fanaticism." Walt shaves the last lock of Ursula's long, thick hair and he runs his fingers along her naked scalp, causing him to tremble with a new pleasure. He imagines pinning her to the wall leaving her no escape, parting her knees with his thigh, and penetrating her, but he knows that will have to wait. They are dressed and perfumed and ready to rally the Inner Circle.

They have transcribed the draft platform from the cocktail napkin to their memories. All through the costuming and head shaving ritual they have been practicing and refining their speech. They have also sketched out an information release that they are looking forward to force-feeding as fantasies to the fourth estate and to Botchi and Botchi, their ad agency.

Walt answers the phone on the first ring. "Yeah?"

"We're ready to start the meeting at the Tycoon."

"Okay, we're on our way."

FILLED WITH PURPOSE, Walt and Ursula burst into the Tycoon Room and the invitees, especially Celeste, gasp at the severe change in their appearance. They march straight front and centre of the Fossil Fuel mobsters who now have taken form as The Inner Circle of ASP, as criminal a gang as ever planned an unlawful enterprise.

Walt starts in, "Nietzsche said, 'Men believe in the truth of all that is seen to be believed in.' So here is what we believe in. The Platform." They all lean forward in anticipation.

"Number One," Walt enunciates, "is The Really Big Lie." To heighten suspense, he peers into every set of eyes. "The feds are going to shut down the oilsands."

Harold exclaims. "They are!!??"

Ursula shouts, "No, you idiot. We just say they're going to shut them down. That's the lie. We tried it out and it went over big at Sunken Coulee, don't you remember?" Everyone nods and looks at Harold. Harold thinks, *my God, my job.*

Walt takes a breath and continues. "You see, Fred can continue to sell this Really Big Lie like snake oil — ASP snake oil — to the gullible electorate." Fiddler nods like a dashboard bobble head. "It's this Really Big Lie that is going to propel us and the party to absolute power because it is going to appeal to every blockhead in Alberia. It's not a big stretch. No voter has to make a quantum leap."

Ursula continues. "The average voter knows that the feds have already imposed draconian emission controls on our oilsands present production. That curtails future development. What we say in The Really Big Lie is just an extension of that … that they intend to shut the oilsands down. The average voter knows that if you shut down the oilsands, you shut the province down."

JB, who has been fondling his duck decoy, raises it in acknowledgement of the revelations. "How da we know the electors are gonna go for it?"

"Mr. Millcutt, the electors are going to buy it, because every dumb shit on the street distrusts the federal government, believes that the feds are out to get us, and is positive that the fed is going to destroy us economically. And that's all we need."

"It's Mailcoat." He jingles the coins in his pocket and

Harold jingles too hoping that JB will see it as a sign of solidarity.

"Yes, we know, " says Walt. Ursula swivels to be sure the seam in her stocking is straight and senses the admiring eyes of Celeste Kinderman.

Fred Fiddler, still nodding, wishes to look engaged. "Yes, besides The Really Big Lie, what else do I have to tell my adoring crowd?"

Walt holds up his fingers as if in a victory sign, "Lies Numbers Two and Three are standard, run-of-the-mill lies. Number Two is lower and fairer tax rates and that sort of shit— "

One of the seriously rich butts in, saying, "That's real important because we're the ones who need the breaks."

"Get this straight," snaps Ursula to the chastised oil baron. "We're not *really* doing this, we only *say* we're doing it. We're taking Alberia out and that's not a lie, that's a fact. But we are not about to lower your taxes. Keep your eye on the prize. The prize for you and your friends is the oilsands."

"The sands, the sands," murmur JB and the seriously rich magnificent seven, sounding like Colonel Kurtz in the last scene of *Apocalypse Now.*

"And you can keep the dead ducks." Ursula rubs her shaved head and her scalp tingles.

Walt clears his throat. "Lie Number Three. New hospitals and schools are fine, whatever, without, of course, increasing taxation, which is always a lie."

Not one word of dissent. No one else wants to look like a dope.

Ursula takes a big breath and continues in a relaxed and celebratory tone. "So much for the lies, gentlemen and um, lady." She shoots a glance at Celeste, thinking she should catch her up on the details of Flossy's hissy fit the night before at the Fizzique Club. "The platform contains a number of actual goodies in mind for the working class. These will be the perks for the people. They shouldn't be afflicted with puritanism—"

Celeste pipes up, "Well, you know what they say about puritanism. 'A puritan is one who has a horrible feeling that somebody, somewhere, might be having a good time.'"

JB grumbles, "That's the guvmint alright. That bunch of farmers." His cronies exhibit their usual silent unanimity.

Walt looks down his nose. "I see you have read Mencken, Mrs. Kinderman." Celeste smiles in self-congratulation. Redirecting his attention to the matter at hand, Walt continues. "Here are the goodies. They refer to drinking, smoking, and screwing. These are not lies, we can make them happen. Consider this vote-harvesting point: we are not concerned with the educated and intelligent, that is, us. But there is a huge constituency of blue collars out there for whom booze, tobacco, dope and sex are the principal comforts and joys in life."

Ursula picks up the ball, striding the length of the Tycoon Room. "If we promise them that their lives shall be less nasty, brutish and short, they shall vote for us." The wait staff and busboys enter the Tycoon to pour coffee and clear the tables but she does not shoo them away. "When we take power, we shall at once lower the drinking age. After all, if a 16-year-old can join our Defence Forces and Security Police and die for Alberia, she or he should be allowed to have a drink! We shall repeal all smoking bans in all venues save for intensive care units. We shall legalize prostitution. We shall legalize marijuana. As for the hard drug traffickers, the death penalty." A current of approval rips through the audience, including the Tycoon service staff.

Walt makes the last, great point. "Taxes from the legalized brothels and on the sale of marijuana will finance the ASP Security Police, our private army." Applause breaks out among the Inner Circle and Fred himself begins chanting "Fiddler, Fiddler, Fiddler." The Inner Circle crowd picks it up and Walt notes that the waiters and waitresses crowding around the door chime in too.

They do not invite discussion. Once the chanting dies down, Ursula says, "That is our last word on the Platform." She signals to the door and adds, "Thank you, lady and gentlemen, we'll adjourn to meet the spouses in the cocktail lounge." She turns and nods at JB and says, "Stick around, JB."

"So what's goin' on?" asks the astute JB, figuring that something is going on.

Ursula delivers the real goodies. "Here's the bottom line. When ASP takes the government, all the oilsands majors except you are going to be expropriated. ASP will own the oilsands and PetroFubar will be the sole operator and the refiner."

"Jeeze! What about my magnificent seven? They put big money into you guys."

Walt calms him down. "Mr. Millcott, they'll be well looked after by us and by you."

"I got ya' there, Bu'ub. And m' name is Mailcoat."

"Yes, I know that."

FOLLOWING the final words at the Tycoon, the participants bog down in the post-repast coffee, port, and cigars in the cocktail lounge. Ursula makes for the ladies cloakroom. She has to check the lay and the symmetry of her filigree silk seamed stockings that go "all the way up to her arse", as JB says to his leering posse. She is followed by Celeste. They are barely into the bathroom area when Celeste grabs Ursula and hauls her into a booth. They exchange voracious tongue-probing kisses, with loud sucking noises in aid. Celeste hikes up Ursula's miniscule skirt and they hold this pose for more than a long, lingering minute, accompanying it with heavy breathing, loud gasping and more sucking noises.

"I see you've kept your old urges, even with that stud poking every hole in your body, Ursula?"

"You always manage to bring out the animal in me, darling."

They separate, emerge from the booth, repair their *dishabille* and giggle and tousle and rub each other's heads, then wash their hands with the fragrant little mini soaps. Celeste says: "Excuse me my dear Ursula, I have to leave to speak to Mr. Semchuk in private."

Ursula replies, "By all means. I expect by this time he is alone in the Tycoon anteroom, avoiding the others. He detests small talk, by the way."

Drying her hands, Celeste, feeling her old confidence returning these days, grimaces her wintry half smile, half smirk. "I think I may be able to keep his attention, my dear."

Spouses have been invited to the Fossil Fuel Club for *après* meeting brandies and the other Mrs. Kinderman, Flossy Megadoll, boings into the washroom. "I've been looking for you," she yells at Celeste. Then, sobbing, she says, "Give me your hands, let me smell your fingers, you cheating, lying bitch."

"Nothing went on, Ursula and I are all over," purrs Celeste to her wife, not quite finishing the sentence that should have continued, "...each other at every possible occasion." This placates Flossy and they give each other little hugs and pecks.

Over Celeste's shoulder, Flossy flips Ursula the finger and Ursula exits with nothing more for Flossy than an evil stare.

"The spouses are joining the Inner Circle in the cocktail lounge…" Celeste says as she steers Flossy out of the washroom. "I have to leave for a while. Matters of state. Have some coffee." Flossy, as is her wont in relations with her butch spouse these days, forces a reluctant social smile, and boings off to join the other spouses.

Celeste knocks on the Tycoon anteroom door.

"What is it?" snarls Walt as he loosens his tie.

Celeste enters the room and closes the door. "I got your message that the investigation of me has been stayed by Baycell Sharpe. Thanks for getting me off." She raises her hand and points to the corners of the room and the ceiling light fixtures, "Are we secure?"

"Mrs. Kinderman, you've seen too many Hollywood spy flicks. You'll find that all your accounts are unfrozen, and the cops sent packing. And after we win the election, for one obvious thing, your…umm…problems will be gone. We'll be a sovereign nation, and we'll own the gold." Walt, with his characteristic economy of motion, signals Celeste to sit in an opposite chair. "You have your uses to the party, Mrs. Kinderman. We value your expertise in certain areas. That is why I invited you today to our Inner Circle deliberations. Now, remind me exactly how much is squirreled away in your Eurostein *anstalt*? And don't lie to me, I have the disclosed police investigators' figures at my office."

"About … I'd say, well it's been a while … with interest, around three million."

"Dollars or euros?"

"Montexian dollars."

"You know it has to go back to the government, Mrs.

Kinderman, but we may be forming the government very soon so just sit on it until I tell you otherwise. Assuming we win, you may wish to donate a sizable portion to the party."

"I may indeed, Mr. Semchuk. I appreciate your intervention."

"Then there is my professional fee, of course."

"Of course."

Walt asks, "All in specie?"

"Gold kilobars."

"How...?"

"I thought you'd never ask, Mr. Semchuk. A long-range jet cargo transport, private carrier, actually a rogue carrier out of Central America. Pre-paid in cash for each shipment. It would re-fuel at St. Helena, no customs, no inspections, no questions, it's not even on most maps or charts, and complete its journey, land, and deliver the cargo at—"

"The abandoned Air Force Base at Arsehold, Alberia."

"Give the man an ashtray. Nothing there but weeds and broken-down buildings and a serviceable landing strip and a provincial reception committee."

"And the Arsehold bunker."

"Yes. All very neat."

"What kind of reception committee, Mrs. Kinderman?"

"Mr. Sharpe looked after those details. Security guards."

Walt leans back in his chair and folds his hands. "Tell me, how did you come up with this scheme?"

"Some years ago I had a client who did the same thing with Candidian uranium, selling it to the FarEasters. I set up his Ordland company. It was all legal, simply an international marketing ploy for dealing in," she winks at Walt, "dodgy commodities, you know."

"Back-to-back contracts?"

"Precisely. Why he came to me was that he was pulling his own differential scam in uranium. It was called overbilling. I thought his scheme was ingenious, so I adapted it to my purposes. He got away with it, by the way."

SEVEN

MAVIS has not been sleeping well and at the time of the ASP platform meeting was in the office of Dr. Travis Zapper, a psychiatrist with a reputation for calming down nervous PetroFubar employees. Reclining on his couch, Mavis' stomach churned.

Zapper dripped like syrup, "What is troubling you?"

"Dr. Zapper, I have this awful recurring dream. An oily duck lurches onto the shore spinning in circles. It tiptoes along the sandy goo, trying to free its feet, it shivers and makes tiny strangled sounds. I know in my dream that's what the last human being in the world will look like."

Zapper replied, "Stop the hysterics, Mavis. Your anxiety is due to insecurity about being in a job that is far too much for you to handle."

"Dr. Zapper, that's wrong. I paid my dues and *then* some down in Tapperlite. We cleaned up arsenic, mercury and all kinds of crap left over from turbo-capitalist copper mining and had successful results. But in the oilsands, fossil fuel environmental destruction makes Tapperlite look like a tropical beach party. Don't you see? Dead ducks are just the symptom. Think about the disease." She howled, "I can't sleep."

"You are overreacting. Let me write you some prescriptions, my dear." He wrote out prescriptions for an antidepressant, a sleeping tranquilizer, and a blood pressure diuretic to spread the wealth to three different drug companies. Mavis bristled at the fact that this fraud of a physician called her 'my dear' and she had to call him 'doctor' when he did not give her the same respect.

Walking right on past the drugstore, she did not fill any of the prescriptions. When she arrived home, she phoned her boss, JB, to find out what happened at the meeting that she missed because of the Zapper appointment. Oddly, JB seemed glad to hear from her. "Missed ya bein' there Mave," he said and added, "drop by my office ta'morrow, I'll tell ya all about it." Mavis wished she had at least picked up the tranquilizers.

Now it is morning, and Mavis tries to ignore the sound of her email inbox as she pops open a can of peaches for breakfast but she can't clear her head of the idea that Nimmo might be in trouble over the recent sabotage attacks on oil pipeline checkpoints. The attacks are too incompetent to be Nimmo's work but she wouldn't put it past the Bos Taurus media to pin them on him.

She takes the peaches and a spoon over to her computer but instead of a message from Nimmo, a notice comes through from the reviewers at the Athabauna Blogosphere website. Her submission to 'Wildlife Links' was rejected, the reviewer claiming that her Owls, Eagles, Trucks and Ducks juxtaposition did not fit the criteria of the competition. "Bullshit," she says aloud, "those assholes are on the PetroFubar payroll just like that prick Dr. Idiot asshole Zapper. Screw 'em!" She pitches her spoon into the sink, puts the half-eaten tin of peaches on the counter top and sits down to re-read what she wrote some weeks ago.

BLOG ENTRY: Athabauna Blogosphere
*"A place for oilsands workers to talk about employment,
bitumen, wildlife and paperwork without fear."*

Submission: Wildlife Links
<u>*The Great Horned Owl.*</u> *Provincial Bird of Alberia. She
executes wide, swooping patterns, listens and hunts, all
senses alert. The owl's incredible sense of hearing, pro-
fessed to be the perfect aural tool and not susceptible to
improvement, misses nothing.* <u>*The Bald Eagle.*</u> *National
Bird of Montexia. The Great Horned Owl's aural capa-
bility is paralleled by the Bald Eagle's visual acumen;
from his swooping prospect he sees a vast, pristine wilderness, desolate and lonely: profuse wild grasses, flocks
of birds and countless wildlife, scrub foliage, muskeg,
and deep wide endless tracts to the horizon of an ante-
diluvian blend of gummy oily tar mixed with rough
sand. These remote, unspoiled and inaccessible wastes
subsist in harmony under the cold smile of the huge
canopy of sky. This is no country for a lost human; nor
for a first human, not for an Anthony Henday, a David
Thompson, an E. Pauline Johnson. This starkly terrify-
ing unknown land is as remote and otherworldly as the
dark side of the moon. One is dwarfed.*

<u>*The Machine.*</u> *Jarringly, superimpose upon this alien
but beautiful landscape a mind-boggling transforma-
tion in the image of a gigantic, filthy truck, taller than
a four-story building, a monstrous wheeled machine of
gross proportions. Piloted by a faceless operator, goggled
and attired like an alien moon walker, the machine
roars and grinds over the roiled, despoiled landscape,*

117

*massive mining and extraction works, great clefts and
intrusions carved out of the muck, giant conveyor belts
trundling black gold to the trucks, huge extraction and
reduction installations, some gleaming like a Star Wars
city, others rusting and decrepit and ugly and frightening, great lakes thick with toxic waste. The sheer colossal scale and extent of these Brobdingnagian industrial
works is breathtaking and intimidating. Again, one is
dwarfed.*

The Duck? The duck is in extremis.

Just as she beginning to feel better about her literary
efforts, in spite of what the reviewers think, an email comes
in from Harold Spincter reminding her of her appointment
with JB Mailcoat. There is additional information that eleven
A.M. is a convenient meeting time for the boss.

Mavis' east end townhouse has the stale smell of a place
that hasn't been used much lately. She roared back from
Athabauna on JB's invitation to get in on the formative ASP
Platform meeting but ended up, instead, panicking on the
Zapper couch. For some reason, though, she feels better
today; more confident about the slow-but-sure success she
and her expanded team has had in oilsands cleanup efforts.
She might even get around to buying groceries and opening
her big stack of mail.

Still in her pajamas, she slides open the big double doors
and steps out on the balcony for a smoke. Cigarette in hand,
she goes through a simple Tai Chi routine to keep the chilly
autumn air from driving her back inside. Between the white-
crane-spreads-wings and the step-back-to-repulse-monkey
moves, she has a chance to think about Sunken Coulee and

the dark side of ethnocentricity. She hopes the stereotyping and prejudice doesn't lead to physical attacks or worse. Maybe her meeting with JB will shed some light on this.

As she is finishing up her routine, she spots Kayla Vandam across the fence in the yard that doubles as the Darktown Riders motorcycle club party garden.

Kayla is strong and wiry with golden curls that are always bouncy, even when pulled out from under a motorcycle helmet. She lives with the ever-smiling and moustachioed Mick Beebe who is the Riders' Bos Taurus chapter president. Kayla is Nimmo's older sister and it was through her that Mavis met Nimmo. Mavis likes the Darktown Riders. They are good neighbours, and provide safety and security to this east-end 'hood. She has never had a problem with them.

Kayla yells up, "Hey, I owe you for poaching your wi-fi. Thanks again, eh?" Besides being the club treasurer, Kayla works as a freelance page layout designer for an oil and gas magazine and has taken to tapping into Mavis' wireless internet service.

Mavis yells over, "No worries, I'll think of something one day."

Kayla is always uploading big files to the magazine but Mavis is seldom at home to experience the internet slowdown. "Just don't be uploading any porn, eh?" says Mavis.

"I know at least a thousand ways to make pumpjacks look sexy. Call that porn? Hey, Mave, you got any pictures of those pathetic oily dead ducks? We're doin' a feature."

"Not the dead ones but I have some nice shots of my PetroFubar science team de-tarring in recovery mode. There's one even got back flying."

Kayla laughs. "You want positive PR? Get PetroFubar to buy an ad, you floozie."

"Shut up Kayla or I'll change my wi-fi password. I'm in town for a while so at least drop over."

Kayla adds, "I ran outta tokes. Can you throw me one?"

"Hang on." Mavis slides back into the condo, grabs a number and shoots it down to Kayla. "Catch. That'll keep you mellow."

Just as she steps back in the apartment her mobile rings a text poke from Nimmo. She smiles and takes a big breath. At least he's still alive and poking. Thinking of Nimmo and their peaceful sit-ins at their last gig, she wishes she could be at his side today for the pipeline civil disobedience rally. She hears nothing but grief from Nimmo about selling out to 'The Man' and crossing over to the dark side but Mavis hopes she can show him that she can make a difference, this time from the inside.

She slides on her cargo pants and Gore Tex jacket, drinks her chicory and heads out for a brisk walk over to PetroFubar. The only concession she makes to her boss' current preoccupation with politics is to don the Inner Circle regulation shiny black cowboy boots. The rest of the ASP costume, which she abhors, is in her closet.

The poplars and cottonwoods are shimmering gold and the midmorning street scene is buzzing with the usual moms in spandex with baby carriages in the parks and bikes and runners along the trails. She is surprised to see red-and-silver ASP bumper stickers driving down the street but they are all on trucks that look like they might have started the day in Sunken Coulee. She cuts down Avenue Mall and arrayed around the windbreak sculptures are the usual motley collection of professional panhandlers. They are not mooching today; they seem well-fed and she realizes from their dress that these are the drop-in shelter recruits hired by ASP for the rallies. They're wearing the same shiny black cowboy boots as is she.

Upon her arrival at the 38th floor of the PetroFubar building she finds herself humming the ASP Party anthem, *Lift up your eyes, To-oo the Great Revolution.* It occurs to her that she'd just heard it in PetroFubar's elevator muzak. She is admitted to Mailcoat's executive suite and hears a gruff, "That you, Mave? C'mon in."

Instead of blustering around drinking beer and jingling coins in his pocket as she had expected, JB is tranquil. Sitting at his hobby desk, he painstakingly applies gold leaf finish to a magnificent duck decoy. Slick is curled up at his side and even though JB has a few flatscreen monitors tuned into the stock reports, the volume has been turned right down. Beyond the wall of west-facing windows, the metropolis of Bos Taurus whines and gyrates but in the sanctity of JB's office today, it is as if Mavis has been transported into a peaceful skypod.

He looks up over his half glasses and says to her, "I carved this ma'self, Mave." He stands up and bashfully thrusts out the duck for her to take. "Here, Mave. It was floatin' pretty lonesome beside yer lunch plate yesterday but gave me a chance to add a few finishin' touches." This is a side of JB she has not seen.

JB's gesture of kindness hits her. "Mr. Mailcoat, I am …, God, I'm…" she says, stumbling over her words. She takes the duck decoy and cradles it to her chest.

"Call me JB, Mave. Ever'body does, even my grandkids down home. Jeeze, I'm glad ya like the bird. Funny about them dead ducks and now this here duck, an —"

Mavis notices him fingering his duck gilding tool as if not knowing what to do with it. She also notes that he is wearing his slimming corset to set off his black designer denims with the perma-creases up the front.

"Wanna beer?" he asks. Without waiting for an answer, he flips open the fridge and starts tossing her a can but thinks better of it, remembering how tenderly she is cradling his duck decoy. Instead, he walks over to her, looks her in the eyes, pops the cap and puts the can down on the corner of his big walnut desk. Pointing at the plush leather visitors' chair, he says, "Take a load off, girl, ya earned it." He leans back against his desk.

She puts the duck on the desk and observes that her fingers are covered with sparkling golden flecks. "Sorry I wasn't at the luncheon yesterday, JB. There was a bad stretch of road about 100 K that ...," She is glad JB interrupts at this point because she doesn't want to go on with a lie.

"I know. Them roads up to Fort Ath are real bad, Mave." He turns and walks behind his massive desk. He picks up the phone, hits a button and barks, "Har'ld, get in here." Now more softly to Mavis he says, "You've bin doin' some real good work lately and I guess I ain't said much about it, but I've had a lot on ma mind these days. From what Har'ld tells me, you and your people are gettin' a good handle on them dead ducks. Har'ld says you need more people and we're gettin' to it." He picks up some papers and shuffles them. "I got here a token of our appreciation, Mave." He shoves them at her. "Here."

She rises and takes the sheaf of crisp PetroFubar share certificates. He says, "Turn 'em over an have a gawk at 'em, they bin endorsed to you. Hang onto 'em, they're tradin' okay now, but you watch, Mave, they're going to be worth a fortune."

She thanks him profusely, embarrassed by his largesse. Not knowing what to say, she stammers, "What happened at the meeting, JB?"

"You won't believe it. Them two spooks shaved their heads, got tattoos, the works. Then they spelled out the party platform."

"You mean Walt and Ursula?"

"Yup, they came up with it, Fiddler's goin' ta deliver it and we're gonna bankroll it."

"Who is 'we'?"

"Me and m' oilpatch buds. We're the magnificent seven. Sometimes we're goin' head to head, like over top leases or somethin', but on this one, we're solid. Thass who 'we' is, Mave."

Mavis is engaged. "And what's the party platform?"

"Them feds are gonna shut down the oilsands." He notices the expression of disbelief on her face. "That's the official line."

"That's the official line? But it's not true?"

"Ya, Mave. That's the Official Lie. The Really Big Lie. That's what Fred Fiddler's goin' to say to sell the party to them folks out there." He waves his hand toward greater Bos Taurus.

Before Mavis can put a reflective lens on any of this, Harold glides into the room with his usual deference. "Yes, JB."

"Har'ld, show Mave where the black Hummer is and give her the keys. She needs better wheels for her Fort Ath trips." He turns to Mavis and says, "Go with Har'ld, talk at ya soon, and oh, and Mave, I'm givin' you a raise."

Clutching her duck and her share certificates, she follows Harold out of the office, but not before she gives JB a grateful smile. They stop at the reception desk where Harold picks up the keys, and they step into the elevator. The muzak is still tuned to the ASP anthem and Harold, listening raptly, hums a passage. Partway down to the parking level, he gets over his annoyance about her getting a raise and makes small talk, "I guess the meeting went well? JB told you about the Really Big Lie?" Mavis just nods as she puts her share certificates into her canvas satchel. She tries adding the golden duck decoy into the bag but it won't fit. She contemplates the gold leaf on her fingers and asks herself a burning question: *Have I crossed over to the other side? Is JB really The Man and am I selling out?*

They reach the parkade. Harold points at the Hummer, gives her the keys, says, "Have a nice day," and walks away. Mavis deposits the duck on the passenger seat, locks the share certificates into the glove compartment, and sets out on a shopping spree. She has answered her own burning question, and she's on fire. She rubs the gold leaf from her hands all over her face and through her hair and takes the stairs two at a time to the halls of merchandise. Her credit card flies from one purchase to the next: Dulce and Babbana stars and polka dot crêpe dress; Mew Mew feather coat; and a Herkes Crange bag, big enough to accommodate a wallet, keys, cellphone and cosmetics. Between the dress and the feather coat she stops at the cosmetic counter for a makeup session and loads up with emollients and mascaras. Last stop she makes is for Ronaldo Blanko stiletto boots but she is careful to have the salesgirl put her ASP cowboy boots in a blue and green striped designer carry bag.

The clothes she put on this morning at her east end apartment she discards in various dressing rooms. Admiring her new purchases in the mirror, she says aloud, "From now on, I'll either be dressed like this or in the uniform of the ASP Party."

On her way back to the Hummer she remembers she had better buy some pantyhose as the last time she wore any stockings was at her Grade Nine piano conservatory practicum. She struts toward Bos Taurus' most exclusive lingerie salon, Sassy Gams. The weather has taken a turn for the worse but instead of taking the elevated walkways, Mavis takes to the street because she needs a smoke. Assailed by a cruel wind, the steel tree sculptures on Avenue Mall emit low moans. Mavis spots the same street people talking in front of a renovation hoarding plastered with ASP posters of Fred Fiddler looking fierce and proud with the slogan "Realize your ASPirations, Join the ASP Revolution." One homeless guy lights her cigarette. She takes a drag, smiles, and opens her green and blue designer shopping bag, revealing her regulation ASP cowboy boots. Then another points at the poster and exclaims to her, "We're on our way, eh?" She smiles, nods in agreement and moves on. This scrofulous core of Fred's private army guards her passage with silent approval.

Entering Sassy Gams, she spots Celeste Kinderman, clad in her usual blue power suit, inspecting silk panties in a display tray. Moments later the spooky Professor Ursula Vere steps out of a fitting room, sees Mavis, does a double take, then recognizes her.

"Darling!" Ursula advances on Mavis and enfolds her in a predatory hug. She runs her hands through Mavis' gold-flecked hair. "Wow, I love your jacket. Are they duck feathers?"

Mavis laughs and replies, "Talk about new looks, I love the no-hair and tattoos. Isn't that the ASP snake?"

"That, my dear, is the asp. It is a snake." She laughs and pulls a card out of her pocket, "Here is the address of my tattoo artist."

Mavis tucks it away.

Celeste, offended by the apparent intimacy, turns and sneers. "Come on you two, break it up. Is this love? Can I be

CD EVANS AND LM SHYBA

the best woman at your wedding?"

As she picks up a sensible pair of nude pantyhose, Mavis observes to Ursula, "I seem to have become a lot more involved with the party lately. I couldn't get to the meeting yesterday but JB briefed me on your party platform." Ursula Vere plucks the sensible hose out of her hand and replaces them with the latest Starlet lace leggings saying, "Delighted to hear it. We need people of your calibre who will be instrumental in guiding the common people to..." she lowers her voice, "believe The Big Lie. We need to get people out to party events." Ursula draws even closer to Mavis. "Can you believe there is already a full-blown Fiddler youth movement?"

"No kidding?" Mavis gushes.

"Remember that neat kid from Sunken Coulee, the snowboarder?"

"The emcee. Tyler somebody."

"Yea, that kid, Tyler Rourke. Walt and I recruited him to head the Fiddler Youth. He's perfect. He was born for the job. All the kids follow him like the Pied Piper."

Celeste laughs and pulls out a wad of cash to pay for her stack of silk panties, "Do you know there are kids strutting around the streets in steel-toed cowboy boots calling Fred's name? Some would call it appalling, others would say it is the end of society as we know it. And some of us will prosper."

Mavis knows JB and the seriously rich magnificent seven will prosper big time. And so might she prosper, which will certainly cover today's spending spree, thanks to her boss. She goes back to the PetroFubar building to get the Hummer and on an impulse she heads for the 38th floor. There she finds JB standing quietly at the window, his attendants gone for the night. He turns, surprised to see her, and is stunned by her cosmetics and fragrance, stiletto boots and feather coat. He is tongue-tied and she marches boldly over to him. She takes his gnarled head in her hands, looks deeply into his eyes and gives him a soft kiss. He runs his fingers through her long black hair admiring the flecks of gold that had rubbed off from her hands. He says, "Jeeze Mave, you're beautiful." She smiles and says, "It's all because of you, and I love the golden duck."

As she drives home in the Hummer through the Bos Taurus sleet and rolling fog, she says to the dead, golden duck riding shotgun in the passenger's seat, "Maybe we should upgrade our living arrangements now — somewhere with a garage big enough for this gas guzzler."

She has not thought of Nimmo for hours.

EIGHT

B Y MID-OCTOBER, Alberia pipeline installations are routinely being subjected to random sabotage attacks. Fred is doing the rounds with speaking engagements and, in an inflammatory speech, capitalizes on the dithering of the conventional police forces: "The Federal Police Service is good for issuing speeding tickets, that's about it." The crowds always love this. He lauds the professionalism of his party's new Alberia Security Police, and the need to take swift and drastic action against "the massed forces of evil against our pipelines."

He calls a press conference, and issues his latest *pronunciamento*, including, of course, The Big Lie: "We of the Alberia Special Party do not back down to fanatics who employ violence and threats of violence. We soldier on, undeterred in our mission. Our oilsands birthright is in grave jeopardy of being closed down, and the current Alberia government is incapable of even protecting our pipelines. The need for an increased security presence in this province is now urgent.

"I say to Premier Svenhardt, whom we gather is otherwise engaged slopping the hogs on his North 40 acres…" The crowds always laugh. "… I say to him, where are you, where is your government, when the people — the citizens — of this province need protection!"

"Translation," says Ursula to Walt whom she has tied up hands and feet to his bedframe, "the door is open wide for ASP and the Alberia Security Police. Vlad, this is perfect." Ursula nibbles Walt's neck and gives him a few playful slaps across the face.

Despite his physical discomfort, Walt presses on about the task at hand. "Professor Vere, we could not have manufactured a more perfect justification for an armed security battalion to be financed by the taxpayers. Our Alberia taxpayers no longer believe that the fed contract cops can do their job."

Ursula runs her long fingers over the snake and blood tattoo on her left shoulder, "Do you realize, Vlad, these tattoos have already been adapted as ASP logos." She unties him and as they drift off together into sleep, he whispers in her ear, "My darling Professor Vere, don't worry, it will please you to know that you will be wearing crowns of Arsehold gold."

THE NEXT DAY, Walt is driving through downtown Bos Taurus and sees a 'For Sale' sign on Mutter Armouries, an ancient and hilarious brick building designed like a Gothic castle with battlements and keeps at each remove and a formidable main gate through which troops in formation can march six abreast. He calls up JB and tells him, "Mutter Armouries will serve well as Alberia Security Police headquarters, and for training and ceremonial parades. It is both perfect and symbolic for our purposes." He adds, "Symbols with which the common people can identify are all important." JB tells him in reply, "I'll get onto it." Walt thinks he hears JB say, "What do you think, Mave?"

ASP issues a call for recruits, and in answer to the call

there is no want of thugs, bullies and floozies now lining up to volunteer for service in the new private militia. They will have to supply their own uniforms and accept ASP scrip in lieu of payment. They are assured by the ingratiating and well-briefed recruiting officers that they shall be paid for every day of service on a time-and-a-half basis, if and when ASP comes to power. This is good enough for the host of the louts and lunks, most of them attracted by a sharp uniform and besotted by the prospect of an unfair fight with someone who can't fight back.

"Each one of these recruits has to feel that he or she is taking part in a *bildungsroman*," sneers Ursula, surveying the enthusiastic lineup from her observation post at the east balcony gallery at Mutter Armories behind the Officers' Mess. "Shall we break for lunch, friends?" she asks the touring Inner Circle which includes Fred Fiddler, The Leader. She pronounces the word friends as if it makes her choke, which it does. "The beef dip," another choke from Walt, "is excellent today."

Walt pronounces to the lunching sponsors of the ASP Security Police, "The Teutonic Knights are an ideal template for our own Knights Templars," adding, with a sneer, "however lame our lot in contrast to their fanatic forbears." He and Ursula are both conversant with the military religious orders of mediaeval Europe and Outremer, notably the Templars. "The Teutonic Knights were the blueprint for the SS."

"The important thing," Ursula says aside to Walt, "is that the ASP 'knights' present to the public as armed protectors, as warrior saints. Pass that on to Mailcoat and his Inner Circle." The ASP military vocation is to be an attractive career option for layabouts, the antisocial, and aggressive morons. The ASP military order grants asylum to criminals, thieves, robbers, murderers, and frauds.

Following their initial weeks of training at the hands of some skilful former military senior combatants as well as some retired old hand streetwise cops, the ASP recruits get their spurs, their snake and blood tattoos, and their uniforms that identify them as members of the Alberia Security Police.

In the observation turret looking out over the tattoo stations, Ursula turns to Fiddler and says, "Identification of the ASP police with the party philosophy is very important, Fred, very significant."

"I should prefer to be addressed as 'Leader', ma'am." Fiddler says with a studied scowl.

"Oh, go fuck yourself, Fred. You're the only one of the Inner Circle taking yourself that seriously." She turns her back on Fred and heads over to review this rancorous exchange with Walt who is observing the head shaving ritual from an adjacent turret. "Fiddler's fat head," she tells him in a huff, "is getting even fatter."

"Calm down, Professor Vere. I should predict that in time Fred will go as batty as a barn owl. But there's no need to be so abusive to him." He sees the dismissive pout on her face. "He remains valuable and malleable."

"Continuing to be useful to our purpose, you mean, Vlad."

"Quite. No one is indispensable. But we are mindful of how much and how rapidly the party is coalescing around one individual."

They turn together to savour the spectacle of buzzing razors and curls hitting the parade ground floor. The upbeat melody of the Alberia Special Party anthem starts to ring through the armoury on a makeshift sound system and Ursula starts moving around to the music, remembering the way they had made the song up right on the spot. "Yes Vlad, I acknowledge the folly of my annoyance. We control Fred Fiddler, totally, don't we? He is dependent upon our feeding not only his insatiable ego, but also replenishing his store of absurd crowd-moving commonplaces, and force-feeding him his clever lines."

"Well done, a quick study you are, as always. Fred is about as independent as a lemming. We have programmed Fred for his meteoric rise to inspire our revolution."

Ursula, mindful of their public perch, backs Walt up against a brick turret and sways side to side to the silly anthem, further fracturing the lyrics, "*Lift up... your dick to my pussy's sol-uu-tion.*"

"I would, but not in front of the troops, my lusty Professor Vere."

A COLUMN of military marchers snakes east from Mutter Armouries on Ninth Avenue, as disreputable a gang of thugs and rogues as has been assembled since the Munich Beer Hall putsch. The word has gone out through the ASP's efficient communication channels to the petty criminals, bar brawlers, assorted garden variety toughs and bullies, aggressive mental defectives, spouse beaters, callow clerks with delusions of grandeur who long to wear a uniform and strut about in jackboots, and assorted sadists — all characterized by their low brows, disfigured noses, loose or weak mouths, and miscellaneous lurid scars. These men and women make up the ASP Volunteers. ASP has, among other thefts, adopted and co-opted the controversial Second Amendment to the Montexian Constitution: "*A well regulated Militia, being necessary to the security of a free State, the right of the people to keep and bear Arms shall not be infringed."*

ASP Inspector Luther Ballast has supervised the issuance of ordnance from the ASP weapon lockers to the volunteers: a stout wooden baton with metal tip, one each; one combat knife. They are not, as yet, issued firearms, which are still on order. JB has decorated his beaver cowboy hat with the ASP rosette, and is sporting a red team leader sash, like that affected by the ASP sergeants, this office conferred upon him before the March For The Freedom of the City, by Fred Fiddler himself, "for conspicuous service to the Party." He is deployed on the steps of City Hall, together with their leader and the Inner Circle, all in the party dress code, to take the salute from their private army. JB, bereft, looks around for Mavis.

The parade deployment of the volunteers is organized and efficient. Many of the non-coms are men and women accustomed to giving orders and ensuring they are carried out 'without any bullshit'. The commissioned officers are all the usual ramrod-backed blockhead species, also culled from retirement and redundancy ranks. Inspector Ballast is a stand-out exception.

Fred, the Supreme Commander-in-Chief to head up the receiving dignitaries and return the troops' salute, is ordered by Ursula to "get out there and look commanding, like you're in charge. A lot of people will be watching this." She knows that once Fred's ego is massaged he exudes confidence.

A lot of people will be watching this because the electronic and print media, notified at a strategic point in time, with a clean sweep assured, are already at City Hall environs for great photo ops. The more aggressive are already arriving in helicopters, like angry hornets, sweeping low to get the view of the route march from the air, then landing and disgorging mike-toting hucksters and cameramen, all eager for Watergate.

Fred is wearing athwartships a ridiculous Napoleon-style tricorn helm sporting the ASP colour cockade, with a flashy scarf in the ASP colours draped over his black suit like a beauty queen. He has a shiny brass telescope under his arm.

Ursula gasps with delight. "Fred has a fucking telescope!"

"An indispensable accoutrement, Professor Vere, for a megalomaniac battlefield commander."

"Oh, it is too humorous, Vlad! Next thing, he'll attend the Bos Taurus Opera wearing a top hat and tails."

"Oh, surely. And a set of rented or stolen war medals."

The ASP march in victory parade to City Hall is in solidarity with its political leaders. Traffic is re-routed; barricades are erected. The city fathers, fearing mayhem, have denied the militia a permit to parade to City Hall, and have alerted the police. The federal contract police and the Bos Taurus Police Service tactical squads, replete with riot gear, are dispatched to disperse them.

The volunteers have wheeled to the front of City Hall, saluted, and are preparing to do their march past.

"Here come the fed cops," laughs Ursula, "late and dilatory as always, but great timing for us." Several fed squad cars, sirens wailing and emergency lights flashing, wheel into the area. They screech to a stop, uniformed cops and a few hurriedly rounded-up tactical squad members leap out, stop, then mill about, wondering what to do next. The ASP Volunteers are ordered to stand at ease in two squads, the marker of each squad, being the tallest member, displaying the squad's battle colours, the two non-coms per squad out front, and the officer of the squad in front of them. The Officer Commanding, a former passed-over army major, bawls to the volunteers: "Volunteers, at ease! Volunteers, ten'shun!!" The volunteers sparkle at parade attention. The cameras roll, recording the evening news, not just in Alberia, but nationally, internationally.

A rather diminutive fed cop individual, inspectors' pips up, commissioned officers' cap badge, steps forward from the gaggle of cops standing on the sidelines, without military punctilio. She is handed a megaphone by an underling, pulls out her Pocket Criminal Code from her forage jacket, cannot open it with one hand, and gestures at the underling. The book is opened by him to the page with the sticky, and held up to her orbs peering through thick eyeglass lenses. She croaks out: "This is an illegal assembly…uuh… unlawful and illegal…uhh, umm…. Twelve or more persons are…." She pauses and squints, the officer holding the Code points to a paragraph with his finger and she continues, haltingly, "… unlawfully and riotously assembled…uhh… here… together. As the lawful agent designate of the Sheriff of this Judicial District…" The underling shakes his head, and points at the book "… as the lawful Deputy, I mean, I am satisfied that a riot is in progress, I command 'silence'!"

There is not a sound. The watching crowd, its ranks swelled, are quiet, waiting to see what happens next. The ASP Volunteers remain at attention. It is Fred's moment. At a nod from Walt, he marches toward his troops. The cops look on, some in awe. Fred Fiddler had successfully defended many a cop in trouble over many years. They revere him. The hapless fed cop inspector continues as Fred marches past her and halts in ludicrous military fashion in front of the officer commanding the ASP Volunteers. The officer commanding draws a ridiculous sword.

"That's a dangerous weapon," the inspector cries, "for a purpose... a p-p-p-purpose dangerous to the public p-p-peace. Arrest that man!"

Not one cop, not one tac team member, moves.

The officer salutes Fred with his sword. Fred raises his idiotic hat, his face set in his "My God, war-at-any-moment" forced look.

"Sir, I report my men on parade."

"Yes. Thank you, Major." Fred addresses his troops. "Men, women, of the Alberia Security Police Volunteers. You are the pride of the force, the cock of the walk! Well done, each and all!"

The officer commanding raises his voice: *"Three cheers for Der Fiddler! Hip-hip—"*

"Hooray!!"

"Hip, hip"'

"Hooray!!" Then *"Fiddler, Fiddler, Fiddler—"*

This choreographed ceremony drowns out the struggling, stammering fed cop inspector, as she hokes and chokes on: "You have disturbed the peace tumult ... tumourult ... timorult."

"A poor bumpkin," observes Ursula, "The fed cops, in my experience, always kick their incompetents upstairs, and eat their own best young."

The besieged inspector has paused, embarrassed. There is some good-natured scoffing from the ranks of the volunteers. The regimental sergeant major growls, "Keep silence! Sergeant, take that woman's name!"

"Her Majesty the Queen charges and c-commands all persons being assembled to disperse and p-p-p-peaceably to depart to their... habit ... habitude ... habitations or to their lawful business on the pain of being-g-g-guilty of an offence for which, on conviction, they may be sentenced to imprisonment for l-l-life."

Fred lifts his hat up to his troops, turns an almost creditable about-face, marches up to the surprised fed cop inspector and doffs his silly hat.

The inspector falls back, ashen-faced. "This is an il-il-illegal assembly …. You have disturbed the peace tumult … tumult —"

"Tumultuously?" Fred finishes for her. His troops burst into affectionate applause, joined by a number of the police officers.

The inspector, red-faced, to Fred, "You're all under arrest!" then blusters over her shoulder, "Sergeant, arrest all these people!"

Dead silence. No movement. The cops stand fast.

"Can ya' b'leeve that?" JB has found Mavis Wong and she stands now at his side.

"Yes, I am perfectly capable of believing that, Mr. Millcott," says Walt. "This is the breakthrough that we have all been planning from day one."

"It's Mailcoat and I wasn't talkin' to you."

Instead of charging the Alberia Security Police ranks, who are itching for a street fight, many of the cops drop their riot weapons and riot shields, doff their helmets, and push forward to embrace the ASP Volunteers, some to join their ranks.

The greedy media cameras record these unusual events. The headlines scream: *Spectacular display of coolness, courage and coordination* and *Cops refuse to intervene* and so on. The incident is aired on all major international networks.

"Friends," Walt intones at the Inner Circle post-mortem, "ASP is now the *de facto* government of Alberia. Roll on the election."

Premier Svenhardt is forced to make a statement: "We cannot have illegal armed militias roaming our land and taking over our streets and exercising arbitrary power. I am calling an election. I have dropped the writ. Let the people of Alberia decide."

NINE

KAYLA VANDAM bangs on Mavis' condo door, yells *Helloooo,* and walks right in. She finds Mavis engrossed, eyes glazed, playing a retro version of *Wolfenstein 3D.* "Grab the other controller, Kayla. I dare ya! This is the level where the *Staatmeisters* wipe out the undead mutants in Castle Hollehammer. Shoot all the giant rats and you can end the biological war."

Sounds of videogame gunfire fill the room. "Mave, you're on fire," Kayla shouts as she crosses the room over to Mavis, pretending to dodge bullets along the way. "Hey, what's with the Hummer and …," she stares down at Mavis' shoulder, "… what's with that badass tat, girlfriend?" She plunks down beside Mavis and starts peeling back the sleeve of her black cowgirl shirt to check out the tattoo.

"Jeeze Kayla, that tickles," Mavis squeals. She pauses the game, puts down the controller, pops the pearl snaps and pulls her arm out of the shirt, "You mean this? This is stage one of the ASP logo, Kayla and it's *supposed* to be badass." She traces the outline of the snake coiling out of her bosom. "Colour gets added in the next go-round and the dripping blood. Hummer is JB's."

"Wicked truck! When are you heading out to the oil-fields?" Kayla asks as she tucks her lanky frame up on the couch beside Mavis and picks up the precious golden duck from its resting roost on Mavis coffee table. Mavis reaches out, plucks the duck from Kayla's grasp and sets it back down on the table, answering the question. "Not goin' back up to Fort Ath anytime soon because the big ASP rally is coming up."

Kayla leaps on the opportunity in a flash. "You got extra tickets by any chance? Mick and me couldn't even score media passes through the magazine — been sold out for ever. I hear Fred puts on an awesome show."

Mavis nods and pulls two tickets out of her pocket. "Here's a couple of centre yard line seats. You guys will be sitting with my PetroFubar ES crew."

"Mave! You are the best." Mavis smiles. Kayla continues, "Who are *you* going with? Probably not my brother? I guess not with that bunch." Kayla jumps up and sashays around the room, "*Doc Mave and Doc Nimmo sittin in a tree, k-i-s-s-i-n-g.*"

Mavis throws a cushion at her.

Kayla says, "Hey, I thought you and Nimmo were going places." She sits down on the corner of the coffee table and lowers her voice. "Speakin' of going places, Mave, Mick and I are moving. He's been elected president of the Alberia Darktowns chapter and we're going to live at the main compound out at Silver Lake."

"Oh gee, I'm going to miss you." Mavis hugs Kayla. "That's a drag but good on Mick. What are you going to do?

"I've been elected treasurer for the Alberia chapter so I'll have lots to do. Trust me, I'm not going to be vacuuming the place. Oh, about the rally, are you going to be sitting with us?"

"Nope, I'll be in the Inner Circle control centre with JB." Mavis picks up the remote. "Kayla, I hope you'll stay but there's some coverage about the rally I have to watch." She flips on the news and presses mute. She sighs. "Long story about Nimmo. I still love him but his righteous indignation has made us …" Mavis' voice trails off and she glances back and forth between the television that is showing crews building pipelines in Alberia and her mobile that has just beeped with a Nimmo poke. "Wait. Quiet, here's the ASP campaign ads." Mavis cranks the volume.

An ASP election campaign spot springs to life on the flatscreen, the artful product of ASP well-paid propagandists Botchi and Botchi. Grainy black and white: lineups of shoppers in the rain outside food stores, beggars outside dilapidated buildings importuning passers-by, gangs in the shabby streets; cut to a circle of thugs beating up an old woman; cut to scrofulous sign-toting enviro-vermin decrying dirty oil. Pan across random rioting in the streets. Mavis says to Kayla, "Pretty believable for hired actors, eh?" Juxtapose this now with happy boys and girls wearing ASP silver-and-red bandanas, having a picnic. Segue to brilliant colour, magnified decibels, with Fred Fiddler in full flight addressing political rallies at Sunken Coulee, Alberia, and other locales, audio track of the Oilsands Miners Chorus hammering out the Independent Alberia anthem. *Lift your eyes to the great revolution.* Mavis hums a bar. Final segue to Tyler Rourke of the Fiddler Youth helping a little old lady across a busy street. The campaign's slogan dwells upon the screen: Realize Your ASPirations. Vote for ASP!

Mavis strides over to her closet and grabs a couple of her beaver-felt black cowboy hats with shiny ASP headbands. "Here." She gushes at Kayla. "You guys wear these to the rally and you'll fit right in."

WALT AND URSULA, fresh out of the shower after now shaving each other head to toe, are watching the same commercial ad. "Vlad," says Ursula as she dabs the last of the shaving cream from between her legs, "Botchi and Botchi has a distinct flair for deceptive persuasion. Despite being a couple of clowns they did an exceptional job." Walt strokes her smooth pubis and counters with the observation that the idiotic attack ads flooding the airwaves are sugar-coated Orwellian euphemisms. "ASP," he hisses, "is the veritable synonym for truth in advertising." He tips her back onto his black silk sheets, sucks first one big toe and then the other and rolls a silk stocking up and down over her foot cleavage, a move that makes them giggle. The television blasts out news propaganda featuring Fiddler demagoguery financed by the vast sums placed at ASP's disposal by JB and his seriously rich magnificent seven.

THE NEXT DAY at the Bos Taurus ASP election rally, the crowd is anguished with anticipation of the big event, exuding huge plumes of steam into the cold Alberian winter night. Eighty thousand frenzied Bos Taurians are singing and gyrating to the head banging sounds of the piped in music, awaiting the arrival of their great leader, Fred Fiddler. Attendees have been handed out warming red and silver ASP blankets and are given a choice of the ASP logo-labeled beer or a shiny thermos of brandy grog. Many of the celebrants have been priming themselves at tailgate parties. Fiddler Youth are roving from section to section tossing out red toques with big silver ASP snake badges to people who forgot, or were too inebriated, to wear something on their head. On command from the massive stage, placards spelling out Fred's name wave through the crowd and thousands of camera flashes glimmer through the stadium like fireflies in a whirlwind. The atmosphere is festive. People are in a good mood. Many have braved winter driving conditions from remote points to attend the rally but for those unable to do so, the proceedings are being beamed to giant screens set up at major shopping malls, community centres and church auditoriums across Alberia.

In the star's dressing room Fred Fiddler is admiring himself in front of the full-length mirror, approving of his image in the tailored black suit with the built-up shoulders and the nipped-in waist. It fits well over his concealed heated undervest but he is scrutinizing his profile for telltale wrinkles. Walt, cynically watching this ritual, hears the roar of the crowd and remarks, "Fred, the master plan to propel you to power is following the script. Our ASP *modus operandi* has capitalized on the mass meeting, the huge spectacle and the hypnotic effect of music and marching squads. All this building up to you, Fred."

"Yes, I am ready for the people."

"You'll get the five minute and walk-on cues. Break a leg, Fred, and don't forget to play our ace in the hole." Walt takes his leave and joins the Inner Circle in their conspicuous celebrity seating.

It is now dark. In the stadium, marching bands blaring medleys from well-known musicals stamp and wheel and fancy step in their choreographed performance bathed by a sweeping multi-coloured light show. The baton twirlers are out front leading the vanguard with impressive displays of their art. Uniformed Fiddler Youth continue to work the stands, now handing out free hot dogs and pretzels. Others carry flasks of brandy grog thermos refills. The ASP blimp descends with searchlights beaming as a hand-picked platoon of ASP volunteers, resplendent in their black uniforms and cowboy boots, march onto the stage and present arms in an elaborate salute to the crowd.

Meanwhile, back in the barns, Celeste and Flossy are having words while the groom saddles Touchdown, the spirited white gelding they hired from the football team.

Flossy takes a swig from her thermos grog saying, "I don't know about this." The horse shies and whinnies, as nervous as Flossy. The groom lunges for the bridle to control the horse's wildly tossing head.

"You'll do fine, dear." Celeste strips off Flossy's fur coat leaving her shivering in her bikini. "Just remember to hang on and don't fall off. You'll look like an asshole in front of all these people." Between Celeste and the groom they manage to propel Flossy into the saddle. The groom secures her ASP boots in the stirrup while Celeste hands her the huge ASP banner. She says, "Take it in your right hand, dear. You'll need your left hand to control the horse."

Flossy whines, "I've changed my mind, I should never have said I'd do this." The horse rears up and is again grabbed by the groom who says to Flossy, "You gotta show Touchdown who's boss, ma'am. Once you get out there, he'll know what to do." The groom listens on his headset. "The cheerleaders' routine is about done, you're on lady." He produces a starting pistol, slaps Touchdown on the flank, and fires the pistol into the air. Celeste steps back as the horse bolts for the stadium track with the hapless Flossy.

The moment they gallop onto the bright field the crowd go out of their minds, surging to their feet, wildly cheering. Flossy, hanging on for dear life, endures the mad gallop around the stadium and the Alberia rebel yellers speed her on her kickass circuit. The cheerleaders leap up and down in sync, waving their red and silver pompoms.

As the crowd noise dies down and Flossy falls off the horse into Celeste's arms, elaborate floats start rolling into the stadium. Mavis is at the main gate working with the ASP parade marshal. She wants to ensure that main placing is given to the PetroFubar Multicultural Enviro-Fund winners that include the War Bonnet First Nations tribe and Ukrainian dancers. Pride-of-place is given to those business enterprises that have contributed heavily to the party, including oilpatch suppliers, restaurants, and car dealerships.

"What the hell?" The parade marshal is scowling and staring. At the far end of the float assembly area, a tractor is pulling forward a float. One look, and Mavis knows it is not authorized. It is painted bright green and emblazoned with banners proclaiming "World's Dirtiest Oil. Stop the Tarsands." She is sure it is Nimmo. It is his style.

She runs over to the float that Nimmo is commanding like Admiral Byrd. She looks up at him and thinks of all that they have shared, from moonlit evenings at Tapperlite pit to their daily text poking to keep each other stimulated. "Nimmo, you know you can't come in here with that." He leans out over the side of the float and yells out at her, "Get out of the way, Mavis. Think of our pact of morality and justice. Face it, you've gone over to the bad guys." He gives thumbs-up to the young AntiTox acolytes who crowd the float, brandishing signs that declare 'Dirty Oil' and 'ASP are PIGS.' "Suck it up Mavis," shouts Nimmo. "We're the good guys and we're goin' in."

As the float lumbers toward the entrance to the stadium Mavis' moral dilemma is overwhelmed by her new loyalties. On her headset, Mavis gets onto JB. "JB, there's trouble out here. AntiTox is trying to force a float into the parade. There's quite a few of them."

"Hang on, Mave. We're comin'." JB gets onto Tyler Rourke. "Tyler, get some Fiddler Youth out to the main gate and shut down the AntiTox float. Bust some heads if you need to. We're not lettin' those assholes piss on Fred's parade."

Tyler says, "Just leave it to me JB. *Heil* Fiddler."

Tyler and his gang of thugs hit the AntiTox float just as it is muscling its way into the main gate. There is a brief bloody battle. The AntiTox types are put to rout. The float is torn apart. The parade continues.

All is in readiness for Fred's moment. Mavis, a bit torn up, has rejoined JB in the Inner Circle celebrity enclosure. They are all there, the leading lights, Walt and Ursula, JB's magnificent seven, and the necessary functionaries, Celeste, now with Flossy at her side, still shivering in her fur coat, and Harold. Members of the magnificent seven are making a lot of fuss of Flossy for her bravura ride.

The orchestra in the pit strikes the opening notes of the Independent Alberia anthem as the Oil Sands Miners Chorus goosestep in their voluminous and ostentatious boots to their places on stage, and as one disciplined body they burst forth with the stirring anthem. Voices from the crowd are raised joining in, then more, until just about every person in the venue is belting out the Alberia Anthem, Ursula having ensured that the jumbotrons have the words writ large.

There is stomping and flag-waving as the anthem closes. Fred strides in like an extravagant peacock and positions himself at centre stage, smack dab on the centre yard line. He launches into his prototypical harangue, with confidence and total self-assurance. Kayla and Mick are sitting amidst Mavis' ASP costumed ES team. Kayla swoons as she is drawn along with everyone else into Fred's hypnotic oration. Mick exclaims, "Hey Kayla, didn't I see that dude in a forties newsreel?"

Fred begins. "My friends. The illegal federal coalition intends to shut down our oilsands completely. Alberia's oilsands are our economic bonanza. The present government of this province is not a government, it is a shambles." His voice rises now. "They are not protecting you. We of the Alberia Special Party will protect you and our precious legacy. We shall confer unity, renewal, and power to the people of Alberia." His voice soars in calculated crescendo and the crowd gushes with delight. "Ask yourself, why are the feds and the enviros moaning and groaning over dead ducks when our jobs and livelihoods are being wiped out? We shall stop those Eastern bastards in their tracks. And who are their handmaidens in their dirty work destroying our birthright? The enviro-vermins with their own five-year plan to shut down our oilsands."

Fred is in full flight as he unravels The Big Lie and the crowd responds with unbridled adulation. "Citizens far and wide are flocking to my banner! Citizens of Alberia, sanctify our cause with your vote. You ask, what is our policy? Our policy is to take … Alberia … out!" The crowd explodes."We will free ourselves from the chains of this obscene Eastern coalition of commies and lefties." As the crowd yells wildly, the stadium lights lower and a spotlight shines down on the heroic Fred Fiddler, a move that Botchi and Botchi pilfered from the Howard Beale character in the movie *Network*. "You ask, what is our object? Our object is an independent Alberia, our own country, our own nation." Cheers and rebel yells from the crowd. "A nation that owns a resource that is the envy of all the nations of the earth. The oilsands." An eruption of cheers. "The oilsands must be ours to develop, ours to exploit, for all Alberians, not to be shut down by those who would ruin this country." As the spotlight follows him strutting and fretting back and forth upon the stage, Fred stops, dead centre, drawing himself up to his full accusatory visage with the pointing finger. "And make no mistake, this is what they plan to do. Shut them down. They want to shut them down, all over a few dead ducks. My friends, when elected, ASP will implement policies to exploit the oilsands without constraints or restrictions. Progress at all cost."

Fred is transported by crowd adulation. He holds up his hands, drops them to applaud his own audience, then holds them up again for quiet. There is a gradual subsidence of foot stomping. There is intense, engaged anticipation.

"You ask, what is our platform. First, forthwith upon our election, we shall issue the Alberian Declaration of Independence. Second, we shall announce unrestricted development and exploitation of our oilsands. Third, we shall expand and enable the Alberia security police to protect our citizens and our industrial installations." He pauses. "And we will drive those parasitical enviro-vermin from our borders.

"You may ask," he continues, "what is our economic policy?" Lowering his voice he pronounces the policies to a hushed crowd. "Meaningful employment for all Alberians, fair and reduced taxation advocating the free market as the engine for growth." Fred takes a studied pause for reflection and he raises his arms into the air and announces Walt's ace in the hole. "And, there will be a $400 cheque in the mail to each and every Alberian every six months starting on the day we are elected."

A tumultuous thunder howls out from the walls of the stadium meeting up in the cold night air with howls through the valleys from every crowd gathered around every big screen at shopping malls and church community halls across Alberia.

"My friends," Fred tones things down to make his final impression. "Let us embrace the real world of the twenty-first century. We do not shirk doing what has to be done. We shall legalize prostitution and marijuana and with the money generated by those enterprises, we shall build hospitals and schools."

In the stands, Mick gives Kayla a nudge. "What's he sayin'? Legalizing this shit is bad for business."

Kayla smiles and gives him a big bear hug under the cozy blanket, "Mick, mark my words, there'll be something in this for us."

Back on stage, Fred Fiddler places his palms together, then holds both sides of his noble forehead — a man, a leader, a born leader, a brave leader, in the deepest personal pain. He straightens, scowls his trademark look of withering con-demnation, and raises his arms. "My dear friends, we shall be citizens of a free Alberia. We shall be citizens of an inde-pendent Alberia. And Alberia, independent Alberia, will not allow our oilsands to be sabotaged by those Eastern bastards, those scrofulous enviro-vermin! We, of ASP, when we take power — when you place us in power, my friends, with your support — we shall pursue our aims and your interests with the greatest harshness!"

The whole stadium erupts in mindless idolatry, wave after wave of hand clapping, foot-stomping, cries, screams, Alberia rebel yells, people jumping up and down, strangers embracing neighbours, everyone on their feet.

"The greatest harshness," Ursula whispers to Walt, "was Hitler's admonition to the general staff on the eve of his blitz-krieg attack on Poland." The Inner Circle look at each other with subdued and smug expressions of self-satisfaction.

Fred recreates his now-predictable *dénouement*, which has been tested in every electoral venue in Alberia. He stretches up, brings his hand across to his chest and raises his noble chin. He spreads his arms high and wide and delivers his trademark shameless plagiarism:

All free persons, wherever they may live,
Are citizens of Alberia.
And therefore, as a free man,
I take pride in the words
"Ich bin ein Alberian!"

Just as Fred reaches his crescendo, Flossy and Touchdown come charging back out onto the track and the crowd screams and glows with the cloying aura of superiority. ASP cheerleaders race back into the field, pompoms flying as spectacular red-and-silver fireworks rocket into the air, letting out bangs and screaming whistles of fire. The crowd is struck, goggle-eyed and panting amidst the pyrotechnics and the descending cascades of multi-coloured smoke. Fred spins on his heel and with a final wave to the crowd, strides off the stage. People are inspired and, as Walt knows, ready to cast their votes for ASP.

TEN

WALT AND URSULA have ducked the limelight and are savouring the election returns in the power-brokers' Tycoon Room while Fred is out in the ballroom of the Fossil Fuel Club giving his victory speech. The results of the vote are an overwhelming plurality to ASP: seventy-five seats are assured of a total eighty-three in the legislature. Svenhardt's fragmented former government has hived off a few obscure seats in forgettable corners, and the one lone socialist member, Fabiola Monk, is returned by a constituency noted for derelict buildings containing artists' lofts.

Fred's triumphant entry into the ballroom and his bombastic, haranguing victory speech are to be remarked by history: "Now Alberia shall stand proudly alone! Now Alberia shall be independent! Alberians have spoken! I shall found a university … I shall build hospitals—" *etc. etc. ad nauseam.* A puffed-up JB stands behind *Der* Fiddler.

Fred's election upset is so stunning, with such a huge margin, and propelling forward such a radical right-wing agenda, that it has not only dominated Candidian and Montexian headlines and reports, it has also excited a huge and various body of foreign reportage and comment.

Exclaims Ursula, "How hideously embarrassing Fred can be. I want a bag on my head."

Walt pauses a moment to gauge his adverse reaction to her outburst. Looking down at his feet he says, "I believe we have succeeded beyond our wildest dreams, Professor Vere," he looks up, "but saying you want to put a bag on your head is downright callous." Walt has not forgotten the long history he has shared with Fred Fiddler.

"Oh, don't be so sensitive, Vlad." She sneers as she glides over to the ice bucket and reaches for the bottle of chilled high-end champagne that she has ordered, the priciest one on the menu. "Congratulations are in order." She pops the cork with ridiculous flourish, pours two crystal flutes and admires the tiny bubbles. "I'm completing an essential riding-by-riding summary for my report to The Inner Circle. That crowd of criminals and degenerates is no doubt toasting their inheritance of the oilsands as we speak. They'll get the oilsands, we'll get the Arsehold Gold."

"Well, no doubt." Walt holds up his glass to hers. "Anyway, here's to our inheritance of the gold." Ursula's snappy ASP regulation uniform is supplemented by the hint of a lace thong garterbelt peeking alongside her ASP snake belt buckle.

THEIR NEXT-DAY MEETING in the Premier's office with *Der* Fiddler is perfunctory. Fred is animated, swollen with self-love, striding back and forth behind his new desk. "I want the following done right now! Action this day—"

"For God's sake, cool it, Fred. Before we hatch your master five-year plan to change the universe, let's address my plan to control it. Yours can wait," Ursula snaps. She advises, "JB Millcott is on his way over."

Fred is nonplussed. He sits down at the premier's oak desk. "I'm not accustomed to being addressed in this—"

"Oh, fuck off, Fred!" from an already exasperated Ursula, "You're in power for two reasons, and that's us, not you. But you did your bit. You did good, kid. There're assholes out there strutting around calling out your name and burning books and giving that odious stiff-arm Hitler salute. But that's just the window dressing. Listen up."

Fred's eyes are wide and he looks over at Walt for support. "I am elected to lead our province with the greatest majority in its history—"

"Something we can capitalize upon, I'm sure, Fred," says Walt, thinking that Ursula's lack of respect for Fred could get her into trouble. He adds, "Well, we can call you Mr. Premier, I suppose."

"That's better. That's better." Fred straightens his tie knot, an unconscious vanity he repeats on multiple occasions daily. Fred's habitual vestment, in contrast to the ASP uniforms of his associates, is his standard tailored dark suit with the pinched-in waist and built-up shoulders. The telephone lights up and is leapt upon in the anteroom by Harold. He knocks discreetly.

"Yes. Come."

"If I may, Mister Premier. It's the Premier of Saskabush. He's calling to offer—"

"I shall take the call, Spincter." Harold vanishes. "Yes? Yes? My dear Mr. Premier…" Walt and Ursula ignore Fred's effusive, meaningless exchanges with the neighbouring Premier, busying themselves with their notes.

JB barges in, "Hey, y'all. How are ya?" He deposits his great bulk into a luxurious burgundy leather armchair. "What's goin' down?"

"The market, but it'll turn around. Fred is patting himself on the shoulder, at the moment, Mr. Millcott," responds

Ursula, walking over and handing him a printed list. "These are the short list candidates for the cabinet of our victory boy wonder. You'll want to look them over. We'll need your input, of course."

"We think that the Premier should name his cabinet and attend upon the Lieutenant Governor with his mandate to form a government, at the earliest," says Walt. JB consults the list of possibles, looking for his magnificent seven. Fiddler is off the phone, basking in tinsel glory.

Ursula says, "Fred, you are to announce your attendance upon the Lieutenant Governor right away."

"But surely the Lord Protector doesn't have to—"

"All in due course, Fred, all in due course," Ursula shaking her head. "First things first, for fuck's sake. We're barely in the goddamn door, and already you want to declare yourself a republic." To the others, "Let's get the cabinet selection under way. Ideally, they can be sworn in and driven off in their chauffeured limos before the weekend. Fred, don't just stand around preening," by now she is shrill. "Get Spincter or whoever or whatever functionary finesses these things to get onto the Lieutenant Governor and set up your appointment." She kicks her chair and a nail snags her stocking.

JB cackles. "Don' fergit ta' curtsey, Fred."

Fred is pissed off. "I shall be addressed as 'Leader'. I have a mind to declare the Protectorate first, then invite the Lieutenant Governor to step down."

"Calm down, Fred, let's solidify our position," protests Walt, "clean out this Augean stable, sock in, hunker down, get our people placed in the right places, get the Alberia Security Police up and running and all over the place and recruiting. Then we can slide in the Protectorate and jettison the persiflage. One step at a time. "

"Get it, Fred?" says Ursula, examining the run that is starting to ladder up the foot of her right stocking.

"I'm all fer thet," says JB, "Sounds like a plan."

Walt winces as always at JB's commonplaces. "Well, come on, Fred, get your ass over to the Lieutenant Governor." Fred, piqued, presses a button on his desk and Harold glides in again. Ursula squirms, looking quite pale, and extracts a bottle of clear nail polish from her official ASP handbag.

As he lumbers by, JB says, "Well, Har'ld, seems ya' got a better job." Walt has told JB that his whipping boy would now be the Premier-Elect's whipping boy, with PetroFubar Energy continuing Harold's salary and perquisites. "Quite a operator, that ther Semchuk," Mailcoat concedes, "Thass politics, I guess. Jeeze." Harold departs with a delicate nod in the direction of his old boss. Harold then makes the necessary calls, confirms the appointment with the Lieutenant Governor at ten o'clock the next morning, and notifies the press corps.

"Okay," says Walt, all business, moving to the conference table, "Let's get to the wooden cabinet. We'll finalize the list by tomorrow afternoon, notify the nominees, arrange the swearing-in for Friday morning." With frowning purpose, they set to as Ursula frantically shellacs the run on her inner ankle with a coat of clear polish.

ON THE legislature steps, Premier-Elect Fiddler announces his cabinet chosen by Walt Semchuk, Ursula Vere, and JB Mailcoat. The nominees, hastily assembled, preen and mug before the tame array of media mikes and cameras. Fred makes some meaningless noises about these qualified and impressive personages who have been hand-picked to serve the people of Alberia in the new era that has dawned, the

Oilsands Miners Chorus is on hand to belt out The Alberia Anthem, and so on.

Two principal portfolios, one of them a phantom, are handed out as well before the other prospects even get a telephone call: Walt Semchuk and JB Mailcoat. JB is appointed Acting Deputy Premier and Minister Without Portfolio. This hollow accolade gives him a seat in cabinet and no responsibilities.

"Kinda a shitty payoff," is JB's response.

"We have explained this to you before, Mr. Millcott," says Walt. "ASP is going to nationalize the oilsands. All the majors except PetroFubar will be expropriated. And PetroFubar will be the operator and your Montexia refineries will handle the product. You don't need a high profile portfolio. You'll have plenty of say, and plenty to do."

"You mean, do I mind bein' th' goat? She-itt, Bu'ub, if th' money's right, I'll grow horns."

"We have a couple of undertakings to which you are well-suited, Mr. Millcutt."

"It's Mailcoat."

"Fair enough, Mr. Mailcoat, and it's Mr. Semchuk."

Ursula sneers, "You'd make a good goat, Mr. Millcutt."

"Professor Vere," breaks in Walt, "our colleague's name is 'Mailcoat.'"

Ursula, taken aback by Walt's public reprimand, continues: "Alright, Mr. *Mailcoat* here. I assume you will be accepting your responsibilities without complaint."

JB asks Walt, "What portfolio does she hold, exactly?"

"She is a Minister Without Compunction, exactly."

Other cabinet heavyweights include Walt Semchuk as the *de facto* Deputy Premier and an ex-cop and ASP insider, George Bilge, as Minister of Police. Ursula declares, "He's ruthless and a street fighter. Just the sort of nasty bully we need. Our militia under his efficient rule should attain a competent level of organization and function." As part of his tasks, Bilge will be expected to recruit ASP Vigilantes who will be Fred's special guards.

Under Bilge, the long-serving Baycell Sharpe becomes Deputy Commander of the Alberia Security Police and the Vigilantes. "He remains the Deputy Attorney General. Sharpe is now the most powerful civil servant in the Fiddler administration," Walt advises Ursula.

Ursula responds, "All in accordance with the divine plan, dear Vlad, considering that he is our principal ally in matters gold. The first steps in making history, Vlad," Ursula continues, "is for Premier Fiddler to declare Alberia an independent nation and institute a state of emergency."

"Quite," says Walt, "I couldn't agree with you more."

Later that day, Walt and Ursula meet with Fred Fiddler in his legislature office for several trying hours, coaching him on his forthcoming public announcements of the Declaration of Independence and the imposition of a state of emergency. After some futile briefing, Fred is on his feet, declaiming: "My friends, our new country is threatened by menaces from within and without!"

Ursula throws up her hands. "Oh, for fuck's sake, Fred, come up with something believable." She looks to Walt for support. "You can't just wave your arms wildly at bogeymen out there."

"Fred, please listen," says Walt, "Try this. 'Intelligence sources' have uncovered a federal plot—"

"Intelligence sources, Walt, what intel—" asks Fred.

"Fred," grates Ursula, "Who th' hell cares! It's fucking *fiction*, Fred. Okay, forget the intelligence sources." Both Fred and Walt look downcast. "Just say this: 'We are aware that the federal government and foreign governments are sponsoring armed enviro-vermin who plan sabotage and vandalism against our oilsands.' And then lay one of your patented looks on them. 'I have to protect Alberia's peaceful and law-abiding citizens.' That's it, Fred. Can you get it right?"

"Fred." Walt lowers the volume in a conciliatory manner, "With the imposition of a state of emergency, here's what happens: there'll be an eleven P.M. curfew; 'threats to security' go before the Special Peoples' Court; public gatherings for purposes other than communal recreation or rallies supporting the party are prohibited; civil liberties are temporarily suspended; protest demonstrations and sit-ins are deemed to be 'armed insurrections'; our ASP Police get extraordinary powers of arrest and detention, as well as immunity. Single party rule is assured. That's what happens, Fred."

ALL IS IN READINESS at the opulent Philharmonia Hall, with its ornate goldleaf rococo appointments now hung with ASP banners and symbols and signs and blown-up photographs. It is an appropriate gilded launchpad for the Alberia Unilateral Declaration of Independence.

"Christ on a Crutch!" Ursula smirks, aside to Walt as they survey the scene with its frantic last-minute preparation activity, "it's almost beyond satire, is it not?"

Walt says nothing.

Official ASP uniforms have been put in the closet for tonight in favour of the *glitterati* equivalent, tuxes for the men and sumptuous black-sequined gowns for the women. At the door they have all been handed a high-class equivalent of the Bos Taurus rally blankets; stunning cross-torso sashes of shining red-and-silver fabric twined with the ASP snake logo. The women all sport their most magnificent collections of Veltlandian diamonds. Ursula has a multi-carat one stuck through her nose.

"It's turning into a Wagnerian potboiler, Vlad," says Ursula, appreciating the way his tight-fitting tuxedo accentuates his physique. "I think he would like to be here today, conducting."

"Well, now that we have our revolution, Professor Vere, now you have your Wagner.'" Walt thinks about pulling up her gown to lay his eyes upon the stockings she has chosen but, instead, finds himself vaguely disaffected.

Arrayed upon the stage are the cabinet and members of The Inner Circle and behind them, Hannah Stroud and the Oilsands Miners Chorus march into place. The Philistines' Philharmonic belts out the *Hallelujah Chorus* and, as at the Bos Taurus Rally, the ASP red-and-silver banners and symbols festoon the premises. All the while, there is marching and counter-marching by the uniformed volunteers and The Fiddler Youth. All are timed and coordinated, tension rising, building to the entrance of the leader and premier of the New Alberia. At a dramatic theatrical point, receiving the appropriate cue on his headset, the Maestro commands the orchestra to full cacophony in the introductory chords of *Also Sprach Zarathrusta*. At a calculated point in the upsurge of this passage, he silences the orchestra with one dramatic flourish of his baton. One can hear a pin drop in the crowded hall. Silence to the very remotest corners of the galleries.

Fred Fiddler, displaying his frowning-concern mask, strides to the lectern which bears the Proclamation. Like the new Alberia anthem, its absurd libretto now put to the purloined *Pilgrim's Chorus* from *Tannhauser*, much of the wording of the Proclamation has been borrowed. Fred, like the rest in attendance, affects a dramatic red-and-silver sash, adorning the tailored black suit. Halting, he adopts his patented pursed-cheeks-mouth-set-in-grim-line face with accompanying-exaggerated-mannerisms, waits the appropriate obligatory theatrical moments learned from *Speeches for all Occasions*, then begins.

"My friends, citizens of the New Alberia, I have here an eloquent document, our Declaration of Independence." The audience applauds. "What this document recites in its elegant prose is that it is necessary for Alberians to assume responsibility for our own affairs and leave the Candidian Federation. The reason? You know our platform. We own our resources. Those Eastern bastards do not recognize that legal right. We have been loyal to Candidia, we have tried in good faith to negotiate with those people. I believe our people need sovereign independence. I therefore declare an independent Alberia." There is tumultuous applause and cheering.

One by one the Premier and cabinet and selected insiders of the Inner Circle affix their signatures on the declaration. The hall is animated with prolonged applause.

Ursula, as she politely claps, says to Walt, "It appears, Vlad, that the Proclamation will assume the significance of the *Magna Carta*."

Walt does not reply.

Fred holds up his hands for quiet. The mob acquiesces. "My friends, in conjunction with this great leap forward for all Alberians, I have no choice but to declare a state of emergency, for the protection of people and state." Parroting Ursula's rehearsal coaching, he says, "I shall not shrink from my duty. We are aware that the federal government and foreign governments are sponsoring armed enviro-vermin who plan sabotage and vandalism against our oilsands. Your government will protect our peaceful and law-abiding citizens and our heritage!"

The hall erupts in ecstatic celebration. Fred strides off the stage, the usual leave-'em-wanting-more *m.o.* Ursula whispers urgently to Walt: "Vlad there couldn't be a better time than this for Fred to go for the triple crown."

"You're right, Professor Vere," says Walt, thinking the same thing. "These conditions are perfect. I'll be right back."

Ursula hisses, "Don't you dare go without me, Vlad!" Together they leap from their front rank seats and make for the wings where Fred has made his majestic exit. Fred is halted just inside the plush side curtain, his hand to his forehead, waxing noble, reprising his moments of glory. Ursula seizes him by the shoulder, turns him, points him to the stage and shrieks. "Get out there. Declare yourself Lord Protector. Now, Fred!"

Walt adds calmly, "She's right. Go for it, Fred. Seize the moment."

Fred pauses, pulls in his stomach and pushes his shoulders forward, fashions his phizzog into its fierce and proud persona, the mouth set and strong, and launches himself back onto the still-floodlit stage. This is his moment! A great roar of approval projects from the crowd. Reaching the centre of the stage, standing in front of the lectern and speaking *extempore*, he orates: "My dear friends. This is a time for healing, but there is much to do, and little time in which to do it, for we are on the threshold of our own greatness for this new nation. For my part, I ask neither honorifics nor emoluments. I ask only to serve you, the people, my office conducted with dignity, and I have nothing to offer but work, work, and more work." Fred is an actor of ability. "I have a duty to the people of this new and brave nation, to their safety and good in every respect. Thus it is incumbent upon me to embrace the role of Lord Protector of Alberia."

Fred pauses, lifting his choreographed face up; he appears to be wrestling with his conscience. He bows his head. The stern, Hollywood handsome visage rises, the mouth resolute. His voice rings out to the limits of the great packed forum and beyond: "I accept this charge and this responsibility, humbly and in all humility."

The floor once more explodes in celebration. "A tautology," sneers Ursula. Walt bookmarks *tautology* in his mind, thinking he'll have to look it up before she springs it on him again and wants to play word pun games *ad infinitum*. He realizes something that he has been contemplating for some time — that she is an elitist and a phony. She is attractive on the outside, but icy cold on the inside and he is getting the chills.

"Shee-it!" exclaims JB, from the front row, "Fred just crowned hisself *king*!"

IN THE AUDIENCE sitting beside JB is Mavis, decorated with a diamond jewellery collection that JB told her belonged to his late wife. She sits quietly, knees together and feet flat on the floor, executing Tai Chi moves behind her closed eyelids, trying to manage her mounting anxiety. *Breathe .... Zouyou Yema Fenzong, part-the-wild-horse's-mane ... Breathe ... Baihe Liangchi, white-crane-spreads-its-wings ... Breathe ... Zuoyou Loux Aobu, brush-knee-and-step-forward.* Between the moves the chatter in her mind shocks her with the seriousness of what is going on in the auditorium and Fred up there on stage; the dictator with his goose-steppers. All she has to do is open her eyes to see for herself what Nimmo used to warn her about — fascist governments and how easy it is for them to legitimately come to power in a democracy. *Breathe ... Shouhui Pipa, Strum-the-lute ...* Alberians have become flustered, as by a rising star that burns out at zenith and have become mesmerized and co-opted, not by Hitler or Stalin, but by ASP's very own homegrown dictator Fred Fiddler. His fervent followers come from all walks of life, from all demographic groups in Alberia, from every stratum of society, from the lowest to the highest. Like Nimmo used to argue in his rants about human morality and ethics, almost everyone harbours warring elements of decency versus toxicity, of altruism versus self-interest, and the adroit ruthless manipulator can unlock that key to the basest instincts that lurk beneath the civilized veneer of all of us. Just like Fred and those spooks Ursula and Walt who run him are doing right now... *breathe ... Zouyou Daojuan Gong, step back and drive monkey away....* Once in power, how will ASP survive? Fred's spooks have studied the horrifying tactics enforced by that monster Adolf Hitler. Fred has convinced everyone that we are at grave risk from vicious and destructive outside rogue elements, designating AntiTox types and the Candidian fed as "hate targets." He has also convinced everyone that only ASP can protect us from them... *breathe ... Zuo Lan Quewei, grasp the bird's tail...* Next, his bogus state of emergency gives him extraordinary powers to abolish civil liberties and citizen participation in government.

Thinking she might be sleeping, JB gives Mavis a gentle nudge and she smiles back, but returns to the drama behind her closed eyes as Fred rants on about his state of emergency. *Breathe ... Yunshou, Wave hands like clouds ...* For total control and complete survival, fascist regimes will next establish a terror apparatus that is feared by all citizens, as it is both arbitrary and capricious and takes on a momentum of its own. Thank goodness, it will never come to this in Alberia, not with JB in the cabinet. *Breathe ...* or might it be that the Fourth Reich is being established in Alberia this very —

She hears a scuffling in the lobby and opens her eyes wide as the lobby doors swing open. A coalition of rabid civil righters surge into the back of the auditorium, waving a petition protesting what they holler as egregious developments: "Citizens want freedom. Freedom cannot be sown in the soil of a police state of fear, *'the fount of all tyranny.'* 'Lord Protector' means 'Absolute Dictator!'" They are hustled out by tough ASP volunteers, roughed up, their names taken down.

Mavis' last thought before JB escorts her out of the auditorium and into a shining night on the town is that the Fourth Reich is being established in Alberia this very night. *Breathe. See no evil, hear no evil —*

WALT AND URSULA are likewise heading out for the night and they have decided to walk back to the Rooftop Lounge at the Hotel Dilettante, for old time's sake, the lengthy elevator ride giving them a chance to tickle each other's tonsils. Walt thinks Ursula cracks a smelly fart but he doesn't say anything. Her breath smells a bit too.

Once they are seated in a position where Ursula can flash a little leg, Walt begins the debriefing session. "Since we're still on the topic of our revolution, Professor Vere, good call on your part to prompt Fred to immediately impose the protectorship."

Ursula says sarcastically, "Still on the topic of the revolution? In our village, Vlad, we speak of little else." She exhales a plume of Turkish tobacco. It has not escaped her that Walt has not leapt to the occasion of lighting up her Oval. "Of course, imperial pretensions are Fred's recurring wet dream. Have you observed him lately? He's taken to wearing eyeshadow and lipstick. He's even spraying on a fake tan! What a *poseur*."

Walt coughs and swats away her rolling smoke. "Yes, I have noticed his new fopperies." Walt pauses for a reflective moment, then says, "Maybe Fred is lonely."

"Pffffttt!" Ursula hisses, "Lonely? What the hell do we care?" She claws a piece of tobacco out of her mouth.

Walt gives her a press under the table and launches in on their usual game of 'where should we go to celebrate our carnal desires, your place or mine.' She brushes him off, announcing that she needs to spend some time on her own, waxing her cranium. Abruptly she leaves the table, expecting him to pay the bill, as he always does.

The waitress comes by and he orders a double. She says, "I don't think I've ever seen you here without your lady."

Walt shrugs. "I might make it a habit."

The person attempting to travel two roads at once will get nowhere.

— *Xun Zi, 350 BCE*

PART THREE

———

Sweetheart Deals

———

ELEVEN

Ursula's sleek BMW coupé and Walt's testosterone truck crunch the late spring ice as they pull up in front of the Posh Royal residence that Celeste shares with Flossy. Ursula discovered from Fred's EA Harold that Walt scheduled a meeting with Celeste at this discreet location and Ursula is sure she needs to be there. As a justification to herself of why she didn't know about the meeting, she reckons that she must have missed Walt's invitation: after all, they have both been very busy of late tending to matters of the revolution.

"Vlad, darling, I'll bet you have missed me desperately," Ursula gushes as she runs up to Walt and throws her arms around him. "I have some wild surprises for you," she says, running one spidery-fingered hand along his shirt collar while the other tousles his hair. "I see you're letting your curls re-emerge, Vlad."

Walt thinks, *you bet, as a declaration of independence*. He is ambivalent about her. His eyes narrow as he observes her. In the week or so since Walt has seen her, Ursula has added tattoos of serpents and winged medusas on both shoulders — artwork that seeps up her neck and on up the back of her waxed dome. New piercings in her nose, lips and eyebrows display blackened wrought iron rings and the one hooking through her right eyebrow is oozing pus. In spite of the cool weather, she is encased in a bikini top and a ratty, torn body stocking with massive silver chains clamped onto grommets at the backs and fronts of her knees.

"Does the surprise have anything to do with piercings in your nether regions, Professor Vere?" She gives him a lusty look through her kohl-lined eyes and sticks out her tongue — struck through now with a nasty-looking stud capped with a multi-carat diamond. He gives her a peck on the cheek, hoping that her black lipstick and eyebrow pus will stay put where they belong, on her face and not on his. "Nice surprise," he says, without enthusiasm.

Their romance has been doused with acid rain of late and is swirling into the toilet. The death knell, Walt realizes, is partly because of her psycho superiority complex, but mostly because of the contempt she has shown for his long-term law partner, Fred Fiddler. Poor old Fred has to get some support somewhere in this tortuous history making. Although worshipped by the masses, he is the constant butt of ridicule from the Inner Circle, and especially from Ursula Vere. Fred is flawed and vain but not a total clot.

Ursula teeters with Walt along the Kindermans' crushed gravel driveway toward the ostentatious brick home, Ursula tipping precariously the whole time on her stilettos. A peevish barking from pampered poodles erupts inside the house.

"Knowing more about the Arsehold gold will no doubt put us in ..." Ursula starts to say but Walt cuts her off.

"The Arsehold gold is not what this meeting is about today." Walt doesn't feel like sharing the fine details but weighs the pros and cons and decides there is no harm in it. He adds, "Celeste is just the sort of cold-blooded operative to run our revolution's Special Peoples' Court. She likes to throw her weight around, and that will keep the rest of the judiciary in line."

Ursula snaps back, not losing a bit of her edge in spite of her radical makeover in appearance, "Yes, there are still some of that lot who support constitutional rights and the independence of the judiciary, Vlad. All that must come to an end." Walt notices she is slurring her words but chalks it up to her colossal tongue stud.

They are met at the front door by Flossy Kinderman, who is not at all happy to see Ursula, but being the perfect Posh Royal hostess, does not let on. Flossy has substituted her professional Megadoll cabaret costume today in favour of a simple flowered frock and a single strand of pearls. Despite her understated footwear, she still boings when she walks.

"Oh, hello Mr. Semchuk," she says, then looks down her nose. "And I see you have brought Professor Vere. Please do come in. Celeste is on the phone…she is always so very busy." She takes his coat and leads them to her wife's study. The study is appointed in the pretentious Posh Royal grand manner: antique brass fireplace fittings; wine table and coffee trolley-on-wheels, both 'antiqued'; invitations and bric-a-brac adorning the mantel, expensive rugs, walnut desk, antique telephone, green-shaded desk lamp, the lot. Walt notices Celeste is using her JB Mailcoat duck decoy as a bookend.

Celeste hangs up her headset. She rises and to her hovering wife she says, "Flossy, would you be so kind as to bring us a tray of coffee and biscuits, please." Flossy pilots the coffee trolley-on-wheels out of the room, accompanied by an earsplitting squeak, a noise that sets the spoiled poodles off on a predictable ruckus of yapping.

Celeste strides over and shakes hands with both Walt and Ursula saying, "Good morning, and to what do I owe this distinct pleasure?" Ursula grabs her hand, using it as a lever to reach out and plant a juicy kiss on Celeste's lips, leaving them smeared with black smooches.

At Celeste's invitation, Walt gestures Ursula in the direction of an armchair, and sits down opposite. The Inner Circle have all retired their regulation ASP uniforms since the election and Walt looks striking in his tight-fitting Eurostyle suit. A distinct contrast, Celeste notes, to Ursula's bizarre getup. She wonders if she sees track marks on Ursula's arms.

Walt starts. "Mrs. Kinderman, we are here today to speak with you about …"

Ursula butts in, and slurs in velvet tones, "Celeste, darling. What Vlad is trying to say is that we are about to decorate your overblown *curriculum vitae*."

"Vlad?" says Celeste, realizing that Ursula means Walt but needing clarification.

"Vlad is a pet name I have," says Ursula, looking over at Walt.

Walt retorts, "Ursula, you might as well refer to me as Walt from now on," and then adds to Celeste, "excuse me, I will go on." Ursula sulks.

"You are aware, Mrs. Kinderman," says Walt, "that the Lord Protector has ordered that a Special Peoples' Court be established. It shall deal with acts of treason and with traitors, that sort of thing. This will be an in-camera court — "

"That means closed," says Professor Vere in a superior manner.

Celeste says, "Thank you, Ursula, your revelation has been common knowledge for the last 400 years."

The room crackles with tensions.

Walt continues, "The Special Peoples' Court is not required to follow rules of evidence, in order to ferret out the truth. The death penalty shall be reinstated for treason."

"Well, I can appreciate the need for certainty in the application of the rule of law, Mr. Semchuk —"

"Rule of law?" slurs Ursula. "Try 'Drool of Law', which might be a more apt description of the swamp into which you are about to immerse yourself."

Celeste ignores her. Walt continues, unperturbed. "We are of the view that the Special Peoples' Court should widen the definition and concept of treason beyond the provisions of the existing Criminal Code. The Charter of Rights is of course abrogated. Our regime is better enabled without it."

Celeste sits forward. She notices that Ursula is fiddling with a hoop dangling from her left eyebrow. Ursula looks at Celeste looking at her, and realigns her fingers to the rips at the thigh level of her exotic body stocking.

Walt continues, "We are mandated by the Lord Protector to appoint Special Peoples' Court judges."

Celeste, by virtue of a lifetime of opportunism, is adroit at shifting gears. She says, "The new Special Peoples' Court should consist of judges selected for their loyalty to the regime." Then, projecting a veneer of scholarship, she adds, "'The theory of equality before the law cannot be allowed to lead to the granting of equality to those who treat the law with contempt.'"

Walt nods. "Precisely what Fred Fiddler, our Lord Protector, stated in his State of Emergency decree For the Protection of People and State, Chief Justice."

Celeste's cheeks glow red; she turns to Walt. "Ummm… did you say… did I hear you right—?"

"There are hard days ahead, Chief Justice Kinderman. We wish to appoint judges who regard it a duty to suppress those elements who would seek to act against the interests of our new nation. The basis for your interpretations must not reside so much in stale legal precedents, but in the ideology of the party and the public pronouncements of the Lord Protector, as well the *gestalt* and the guidance of the people. Of course."

"Ahem. Ummm. I take your point, Mr. Semchuk. You can count upon my...umm... great experience and discretion, sir ...." She half rises to bow to him.

"The public announcement shall be forthcoming," says Walt. "You will be notified by the Lord Protector's protocol office. There shall, of course, be a formal swearing-in ceremony at the Law Courts building. Underlings will consult you upon the design of the new court's distinctive robing. The Chief Justice's robe shall, of course, bear distinguishing marks commensurate with her high office."

Flossy pops her head into the study to ask if anyone needs cream for their coffee and when she notices the big black lip-marks on Celeste's mouth, she stares over at Ursula. Her eyes are nasty, gleaming little points.

Ursula states, hoping to put the pig sticker into Flossy while she is listening, "Celeste, you know that the Chief Justice of the Special Peoples' Court of Alberia shall" — she removes a Turkish Oval from her gold cigarette case — "rank equally with the Chief Justice of Alberia." She places the cigarette between her blackened lips and looks back and forth from Walt to Celeste and back to Walt, hoping that one or the other will leap up to give her a light.

Celeste's chair scrapes across the hardwood floor as she exerts dominance and rises from her desk. Brandishing Flossy's vintage Dunhill lighter, she strides over to Ursula, takes her by the arm and escorts her to the door of the study. She places the lighter into the palm of her hand with a smack and says, "Darling, I'm sure you don't mind popping out onto the little deck out back to smoke that. The poodles have allergies."

"Mmm. Yes, I see, Chief Justice Kinderman," Ursula says. She turns to leave, but not before she lights the Oval and puffs a toxic plume of smoke into the room. Her stilettos click as she walks down the hall and out onto the deck, where she shivers in the brisk morning air. She sucks her cigarette until it glows orange, the whole time fingering her facial piercings and playing with the tears in her stockings. She listens to the usual neighbourhood sounds and birds chirping back at her as she flips the cap on the Dunhill lighter.

Flossy's coffee trolley-on-wheels comes squealing out of the kitchen, accompanied by a yapping parade of manicured poodles. Flossy stops her clatter and, out of a sense of obligation, offers Ursula a steaming cup of coffee and a Peak Frean. Ursula takes a sip and slurs, "This blend is, sadly, a bit young for me." She perches her cup on the deck rail and then says, "Flossy, darling, I hope your saddle sores have healed since the wild ride at the Bos Taurus rally."

"Yes," says Flossy. Noticing that Ursula has her treasured lighter she makes a decision. She pauses and then says, "Professor Vere, why not step inside? I don't like to see you freezing out here. I often sneak a smoke down in the rumpus room." Ursula sees a chance to get some comfort and follows Flossy down the stairs.

A HALF HOUR or more has passed. Celeste wonders aloud about the coffee and adds that her neighbours must be hacking at their trees again. Walt has turned their conversation to the Arsehold gold. When they hear Flossy squeaking toward the room, Celeste puts a cautionary finger to her blackened lips. "Flossy doesn't know anything about the gold."

The study door bangs open and in staggers Flossy, pushing the antiqued coffee trolley with one arm and cradling a chainsaw, dripping with a horrendous mixture of gore, in the other. Her flowered frock is covered in blood and her pearls have ruptured, leaving a trail down the hall and on down the stairs.

Flossy drops the chainsaw with a mighty crash and starts to shake and weep. She sobs, "Here's your coffee," adding, "I'm afraid I've caused a bit of a rumpus downstairs." She explodes in tears.

Celeste moves towards her but the is arrested by the profusion of blood and tattooed pieces of flayed skin hanging off the chainsaw.

Walt says, "Perhaps, Celeste, we should check the rumpus room."

Celeste says to Flossy, tenderly, "Perhaps you'll feel better if you get cleaned up, dear."

Flossy responds, "I don't want to be alone."

With trepidation, they follow her trail of pearls down the hall and pilot Flossy on down the stairs. They freeze on the last rung. A person they have all grown to despise is now in pieces, strewn about the basement.

Flossy chokes out, "It's Ursula."

Celeste says, "We rather gathered that, dear. What happened?"

Flossy begins, pointing at the limbless torso in the centre of the room, "Well, that's her middle." Walt and Celeste are aghast, frozen. Flossy continues, pointing, "There's an arm over there in the laundry room, and, well, the other one, it's there with the dogs."

Celeste and Walt note the poodles lapping at a fibula. Celeste gasps, "One of her legs is on my exercise bike." Indeed, a stockinged leg has landed on the pedals.

Flossy wails, "There's blood all over my karaoke. How am I supposed to get *that* out. Oh look, there's my lighter." With admirable self-possession, Flossy recovers her lighter. She walks over to Celeste, holds the Dunhill up in her gore-stained hand and says, "Mine."

"Well," says Walt, horrified but relieved, "We have to deal with this."

"Jesus Christ!" Celeste blurts, goggle-eyed.

"Yes, that appears to cover the situation. And we had better be covering this situation, Chief Justice." Walt gets on his mobile. "Tyler? Walt. Got a job for you. Right now. Here's the address. You're the proud owner of a new BMW."

Celeste is all business. "We'll need some carbolic solution and a bonfire, Mr. Semchuk. There's a fire-pit at the bottom of the garden."

TWELVE

I‍T IS THE SAME, only different. Walt's apartment is eerily quiet without the flamboyant presence of his late companion Professor Vere. No shrill ranting, no whiney requests for a quick round of silk-stocking-enhanced asphyxiation sex, no cheap shots at his long-time law partner cum Lord Protector Fred Fiddler. Despite his admiration for her high intelligence, he knows he has been in bondage and in her thrall. He was taken down by a badass dominatrix and needs to distance himself from what he has become.

Revisiting his values, he reflects that he is a good lawyer and a first-rate collector of rare and precious minerals. He believes in the rational versus irrational; logic versus paradox; beautiful versus ugly, and is wondering how far this bogus revolution would have gone had it not been for the evil Professor Vere and her hasty cocktail napkin of Big Lies. It doesn't say much for him that he couldn't keep his lusty passions in check to prevent the aimless path of this revolution that has much more now to do with greed and hitting the jackpot with the Arsehold Gold than with completing an exercise in curiosity about the human condition. Well, at least he can walk away, once and for all, from Vlad, his vampiric birthname.

He will need to redefine his personal interests if he is to

be the captain of his own ship. He has enjoyed experimenting with different styles of poetry, especially rhyming couplets, and the only rhymes he has composed in the last months are those that make up the doggerel Alberia ASP Party anthem —a most pathetic contribution to the canon of popular song. Why did the plan seem so profound and perfect at the time? Was it the way Ursula wrapped herself up in the satin sheet and flounced around with what seemed like perfect grace? Try as he might, he cannot expel her image from his mind.

He rummages around on a lower level of his massive bookshelf amid cast-off or long-forgotten items such as JB's duck decoy and a pair of handcuffs he suspects belonged to Ursula. He finds his vintage Gibson electric guitar, dusts it off with a pair of stockings he finds lying around and tunes it up. He decides to sing a song to Ursula Vere as if she were still right there in front of him, in an attempt to purge her from his consciousness. Not up to creating his own chord progressions, he picks a riff and fractures the lyrics to *Lay Down Sally*:

Pussywhipper, cast me in your spell,
I have made a fascist state to impress you.
Pussywhipper, a chainsaw takes you out
Don't you dare to come back round just to haunt me.

As he wanders over to his old law office, he wonders if Celeste is going through the same thing. Fleetingly, he admires Flossy for her enterprise.

WALT AND FRED, otherwise engaged in running a country, have to dispose of their law practice. They are back at the office. Ingrid has made them coffee and has been taking Fred's fish down from the rafters.

Ingrid says, "The active files are all on Fred's desk. If you run into problems, give me a shout."

As Fred and Walt start going through the files, Ingrid walks by with Fred's honourary eagle-feather headdress. "Fred, you'll want this packed, for sure."

Fred rises and takes his headdress. "You remember, Walt, when we took on the feds for Elvis and his tribe? That was a real victory, wasn't it."

Walt smiles, remembering one of their most successful combats on behalf of their First Nations client.

Fred is reflective. "They gave me the name Wise Owl Spirit, do you remember?"

"Yeah, it got you in the gut. It meant a lot to you."

Ingrid hollers from the next room. "What do you want to do with these wooden ducks?"

"Pack them somewhere."

Ingrid is taking the pictures down off the walls and she reaches up to one of Fred and Walt with a group of fierce-looking bikers. Walt runs over and gestures at the picture, "You remember this one, Fred?"

"Valued long-time clients of the firm, Walt. That's the time the cops hit their clubhouse."

Walt laughs. "I remember them coming in. Mick Beebe had a paper bag full of big bills. That was the retainer."

Fred said, "Yeah I remember, and they didn't want a receipt."

They spend an amiable time going through files and reliving old combats. When they finish, Fred says to Ingrid, "Can you box these up and send them over to the new firm?"

As she leaves, she says, "I'm looking forward to those

guys too."

Walt pours Fred a drink and says, "Busy days, huh, Fred. How are you holding up?"

Fred sighs, hunches his shoulders, and assumes one of his masks. "I have a duty to the people —"

Walt puts a gentle hand on his friend's arm. "Fred, it's just me here."

"It's lonely at the top, I'm glad you're with me."

Walt says, "Well, we've got a big deal coming up, that's for sure. The FarEasters will be here in a few days."

Fred scowls, "Walt, how are you going about taking out the majors and selling the sands to them?"

"Well, Fred, we retain Donald Grandstander of the omnipotent law factory. Let a massive legal mill sort it all out and look at and after the details, and not fuck it up, that's what these deadly sorts of solicitors are paid upwards of 700 bucks an hour to do. You know, Fred, the rent on their clients' washroom alone per week probably exceeds what it cost to rent this dump for a year."

A commotion of whoops and hollers comes from the street below. They look out the window and see the people holding up their $400 oil money cheques, ready to party in the bars. Two uniformed ASP volunteers on foot patrol are cheered by the good-natured crowd.

"They love you, Fred, and they love the party. We'd better get over to the Lord Protector's office."

AT THE SAME TIME, sprawled in his office chair behind his cluttered desk, JB shakes his beer can, "Kee-rist, Mave, I'm dry." He lobs the empty at the wastebasket set in the middle of the room. Clunk! "Hey, made the team, Mave!"

Mavis says, " Hey, Slick, JB made the team this time." Slick wags his big tail, helicopter style, and comes around to Mavis for a cuff and a pat. JB hoists himself up to enjoy the domestic scene, scratches the latches on his corset and hauls himself up from his captain's chair.

They meet at the fridge with a happy look, and help themselves from his stock. "Say, JB," says Mavis as she pulls the tab with a hiss, "since we're sleeping together, don't you think it's time you told me your first name?"

"Shee-it, Mave, I don't have a first name. My folks just give me the initials. But I'll give ya the one on my passport, it's Jaybee."

Mavis laughs at this. JB gives her a sober look, "Doggone it, Mave, ya know I gotta meet up with The Seven and tell 'em what's goin' down. Like it's gonna be ugly."

"Well, I can't feel too sorry for them, they've all done very well." She joins JB over at the window and puts her arm around him."

He snuggles against her, "Mave, you're a FarEaster —"

"Yes racially, understanding my Grandfather helped build the railroad and I'm third generation Alberian —"

"You speak the lingo, right?"

"Oh yes, I can get by."

'Well, we're gonna need ya. The party is sellin' half the oilsands to them FarEasters."

"They are? That's news to me. With the way things have been going with our potential markets, the pipelines choked off I mean, I'm not surprised. Let me know how I can help."

"You can help me right now by tellin' me about these FarEasters. Ain't they commies?"

"JB, FarEast is now *the* world power. The FarEast Communist Party has become the Capitalist Dictatorship

Party. The people running the country have stripped all of the state-owned property and have taken over energy, transportation, its corporations, courts, and cops."

"Sounds familiar, Mave, and sounds like ASP. I think we can do business with these people. They need oil, lots of oil, real bad. We got oil and we want to sell. We're not doin' well in Montexia, with the dirty oil lobby and all that."

Mavis nods. She understands JB's sentiments, but sees, in her mind, Nimmo brandishing his dirty oil sign, and her moral compass once again goes into a spin. She has heard nothing, not even a poke on her mobile, since the Bos Taurus rally.

His intercom buzzes: "Mr. Mailcoat, they're all in the conference room." Mailcoat says, "Come on, Mave. Slick, stay."

JB enters the conference room and lays a heavy upon his Inner Circle of invited larcenous oil company majors, his magnificent seven, heavy into bitumen. "Okay, here's whass goin' down, and yer gettin' a heads up: Alberia, that is, ASP, wants th'oilsands. Like all of it. They're gonna sell half t' th' FarEasters."

"Wha…!!" General consternation.

"Keep your socks and shirts on. Thass politics. Ther ain't no choice, ya'll gets expropriated by th' govmint, wot ya' got is gone, an' yer holdin' is nationalized."

"Wha…!!" Even more consternation.

"Ya'all 'll be well paid. An the juniors don't get no choice: they jes gets expropriated, paid a token. Thass it, take it er leave it."

The room is silent.

"Ya'all 'll be bought out at more than top dollar, so quit yer bitchin' cos th' decision's bin made, right, Mave?" He nods at Mavis and she nods back. "My shop PetroFubar is gonna' be th'overall operator of all them facilities, includin' the FarEaster half of everything. Thass part of th' deal. It's a huge op, so I'm lookin' fer partners in a joint venture, ya get my meanin'? Ya get in on th' ground floor a' that one and make another mint."

The magnificent seven exchange uneasy looks.

"Get some more liquor in here, right now," JB barks at a hovering underling.

"Look, youse guys, we've taken a lotta collective shit, from them feds, them enviros, and them deadheads in Montexia, so th' good news fer you is yer pieced off real handsome; an' still in control — granted, with a partner yer not too fussy about — an' th' sky's th' limit. No brakes on sands exploitation. So think about it. Ya want in on th' operatin' company, I'll sell ya'all shares in a sweetheart deal. Where're those drinks?"

A mean looking son of a bitch in the corner, with snap-down sunshades over his glasses, speaks out. "Listen up, JB, all of us here were in on the ground floor of ASP, we bank-rolled that goofball Fiddler, we're all Inner Circle, we got a right to carve out the oilsands for ourselves. That was the deal. You're dropping a bombshell on us, no warning, ASP is going to expropriate, we're out, but you're still in. Have I got the picture right?"

Murmurs of disapproval from the others.

"And you know what you're doing, JB?" exclaims another. "Getting in bed with them FarEasters, man, talk about giving away the farm!"

"I'm cumin' out jes fine, thank you. Th' FarEast'll buy all our output. Th' product can't go east, it can't go west, y'know, th' feds have stopped up all th' Candidian pipelines out of Alberia. But we can sure as hell go south to Montexia, and guess who owns th' two refineries that will be goin' full bore?"

"And how are you going to get the refined product out to the west coast?"

"Hey, man, Montexia's my territory. We're talkin' JB Mailcoat's town. I got everbody greased from way back. Happens that my country also needs 'lectricity in a big way, and th' cost of them new transmission lines is a bugger right now fer the govmint, not t' mention the shower a' shit from th' landowners, tie it up fer decades. Happens that Alberia got a lot of extra 'lectricity t' sell. All them coal-fired plants are goin' full bore, an' we got coal as well as oil. We can horse trade. So what ya lose on th' roundabouts, ya gains on the swings."

IT IS TWO DAYS LATER. The FarEasters arrive in Bos Taurus. Following restrained greetings, the two parties are arranged in negotiating mode facing each other across the Lord Protector's massive boardroom table.

Sitting on ASP's side are Walt Semchuk, JB Mailcoat, Baycell Sharpe and the Alberia government's high-priced lawyers. Mavis Wong, sitting beside Mailcoat, provides cultural affinity. Behind their seats are assorted functionaries from Energy and from Finance, armed with volumes of briefs and statutes. Harold hovers close to Baycell, for his own reasons of affinity.

The FarEaster delegation are all beaming and well-scrubbed, sitting at courteous attention in identical black suits and white shirts with red ties and with the party's red star in each left lapel. There are identical blue looseleaf folders in front of each member. The row of seats behind the lead delegation is also occupied by their boffins and bureaucrats. They have one spokesman only, an authoritative and impeccably turned-out FarEast gentleman who speaks excellent English. His name is Mr. Ling.

"Ladies and Gentlemen," Walt begins, "I welcome you all to this historic meeting. I believe each party has met the other members."

"Ah, yes, Mr. Semchuk," says Mr. Ling, "We are all acquainted, as you see." There are nervous smiles at the table. "I believe," says Ling, "that all the legalities have been worked out between our respective legal counsel —"

With a nod of his head he indicates Mr. Chan of his front rank and then nods across the table to the hovering Grandstander. Mavis thinks Mr. Chan looks like her grandfather.

Walt leans forward and looks at Grandstander. "Yes, surely," Grandstander intones, "All the details agreed and papered, all as per specifications. There are some provisos, of course, going to the root of the contract. These are acceptable to both sides."

Mr. Ling translates. Then, Mr. Chan, expressionless, manages an acquiescing head inclination.

Walt continues. "Well, then, we don't have much to discuss. We appreciate you have invested in recent years in the oilsands. We seceded from Candidia so we could manage and exploit our own resource. We have nationalized our oilsands. You are now our full partners in this exciting venture, and you will be able to consume our product. As to how we get it to you, I call upon Mr. Mailcoat."

Mr. Ling translates.

JB stands, "PetroFubar Energy is gonna be yer operator at th' sands. We know what we're doin'. I own two refineries in Montexia goin' full bore with sands bitumen. It gets piped straight down south. It don't go through Candidian soil."

Mr. Ling translates and leans forward. "And the transport of the refined product?"

"Once we thin out that ther shit, ther's no problem gettin' it out t' th' west coast. Alberia bitumen's gonna flow down to, then outta, my refineries, then ride out to the west coast. The pipe's ther already, the Donner Pipeline, and gets my refineries' product straight out to a deep sea port south o' Seadle. And don' worry none. The product'll be out to your oil tankers like shit through a goose."

Mr. Ling translates and the FarEast delegates smile.

"Finally," says Ling, "there is the vexing question of the slow pace of realization of the oilsands product that our government now owns jointly with your government."

JB says, "Th' problem is gettin' th' water heated for oil extraction. We got natural gas, but it's real slow, an'…"

"I think we have the technology to accelerate your — our — oilsands production." Mr. Ling defers with an inclination of his head to a compact colleague, expressionless behind large rimless spectacles. "Mr. Wu speaks English."

Mr. Wu half rises and bows. "My company manufactures a mobile nuclear-powered heat source that will accelerate the heating process exponentially. Our small nuclear reactor, a mini-power reactor, is a good match for extraction needs. It operates from a rolling vehicle in remote locations. It is independent of fuel supply chains. It is constructed on site; we can manufacture and ship the modular components. It is very efficient and has proven reliable in our country."

Mavis says, "What about its safety record? Alberians are very wary of nuclear power. There have been some terrible accidents."

"It has an outstanding safety record," responds Mr. Wu, "and our training is very thorough."

Mr. Ling brings the tips of his expressive fingers together. "It would be in all of our interests for this technology to be implemented in our oilsands."

Walt says, "That would be most satisfactory from my government's point of view." He sits back in his chair. "Ladies and gentlemen, I believe that concludes all matters on the agenda?" The spokesman inclines his head respectfully. "Then I invite all persons present to a private reception with our host the Lord Protector, and I declare this meeting adjourned."

All front rank parties at the table applaud each other.

THIRTEEN

NIMMO VANDAM is incarcerated in a converted Bos Taurus warehouse housing persons accused of high treason against ASP. The prison, forbidding and strewn with detritus, is officially named The Peoples' Court Remand Centre but is known on the inside as Lubyanka. Nimmo receives one ration a day of watery soup and stale bread. It is a hellhole, and now that summer has hit, the atmosphere is stifling and fetid. He has not been allowed a change of clothing. He is subjected daily to ragged intermittent screams of his AntiTox colleagues, and other so-called dissidents.

Nimmo thinks back to the preceding weeks. The terse email from Mavis saying *get out, now,* the heavy treads of vigilante boots in the hall of his modest apartment, the midnight knock. Thrown into solitary. Various thugs take turns beating him up. Only then does he find out why he is there. They insist he sign a confession to bombing a PetroFubar oilsands installation. He tells them over and over, *I refuse to confess to something I didn't do, you assholes.*

The next thing he knows, he's being tried before Chief Justice Celeste Kinderman in a closed court. He remembers that this wacko witch keeps yelling at him that he is in contempt. Then some total strangers get up and testify that he was the bomber. He doesn't even have a lawyer. He shouts out, "I don't even know these people." He is ignored. Justice

Kinderman finds him guilty and right there sentences him to be hanged. It is all over fast. As he is manacled and dragged out of the courtroom, he sees his great love Mavis Wong sitting in the corner and wonders how she got there.

He's returned to prison and placed in general population. As he's eating his watery soup at the rough table with other inmates, he thinks of people who are at the table one day and gone the next. A guard tells him *you got a visitor.* The other prisoners stare at him. Visitors are not allowed. Nimmo is led down a flight of stairs to a small interview room and greets Mavis with sobs and clinging hugs. They sit down at a card table on a couple of plastic chairs. She smokes.

Mavis says, "I got into the trial because I was representing the victim, PetroFubar. Insiders are allowed in the court."

"Insiders? Mavis. What have you done? Do you have any idea what's going on out there?"

"My boss is an insider, that's how I was able to see you. He's a good guy."

"A good guy!? Let me tell you what's going on in the street. ASP is a one-party tyranny with a terror apparatus. Secret police, confiscation, concentration camps, deportations, murder. They're going to murder me, Mavis, and it's all financed by the oilsands."

Mavis is horrified. She stammers, "I want to save you. I've got to save you." She drags on her cigarette.

Nimmo coughs, "Your smoking is irritating, Mavis, and your Nazi conduct is more than irritating."

She drops her cigarette on the floor and grinds it out with her ASP-issue boot. "Nimmo, I got caught up in this. I needed money —"

"We did fine without money at Tapperlite. Suddenly you need it?"

"Good for you, Nimmo. You had the silver spoon. Tapperlite was different. It was a different era for us. I have to work my ass off now to pay off my student loans and my boss looks out for me." Nimmo rolls his eyes back. "JB and I work closely and I got sucked into this whole scene. I'm not proud of it."

"Let me see if I've got this right … you became a Nazi to pay off your student loans?" He is up and pacing. "*I'm* proud of what *I've* done. You know, I didn't go around blowing things up like they said."

"That's their specialty, Nimmo, the big lies."

"That's the whopper that's going to kill me. What isn't a lie is what AntiTox tried to do in the oilsands: the surveillance, monitoring, getting evidence, sit-ins and demonstrations — anything to try to build awareness. We worked with the other groups to make a difference in the oilsands because what they are doing up there is obscene. Dead ducks! That's just the symptom. Think about the disease."

Mavis remembers using exactly those words not long ago on the shrink's couch. She closes her eyes, tears streaming, "I can't explain it. It just swept me away. It swept everybody away."

Nimmo yells, "Yeah, everybody but the ones of us they're exterminating. They call us the enviro-vermin." He drops his voice. "Let me tell you about your revolution. These Nazis are all over the schools and the campuses, these bald and tattooed goons. Look, it's jackboots and black uniforms and snake armbands. They come out at night with torches, they burn books in big bonfires, they drag teachers and students out in the street and make them march and sing Fiddler songs. That's your revolution."

With almost a flatness, she tells him, "I know I can help

you."

Nimmo rants, "Look, one guy in here, Tom, I talked to him and he was a wonderful man. He was the president of the university. He gave me these. He slipped them to me. These are his notes of what happened to him." Nimmo shoves a clutch of dirty newspaper at her and she puts them under her shirt. "He told me ASP killed their own Minister of Police, that guy Bilge. He set this prison up. He told me ASP killed Fabiola Monk, you know, the socialist opposition leader. What they did to Tom, you would not believe. Then all I know is they took him away."

She leans across the table and whispers, "Listen Nimmo. Trust me. My boss is going to get you out of here. Trust me and talk to no one."

The guard bangs at the door, "Time's up."

They come out of the interview and JB is standing at the end of the hall with two uniformed vigilantes. The prison guard takes Nimmo by the elbow to walk him away.

"Hold it, Bu'ub," commands JB.

The guard half turns, "Yeah, who are you?"

JB holds up his Inner Circle identity badge, its snake catching the fluorescent light. "Them two people are goin' with me, right now."

Nimmo tries to pull back, but he is weak from abuse and privation and held by the guard. Mavis whispers, "It's okay, it's JB Mailcoat, my boss."

JB says to the guard, "Let 'im go." Then, to Nimmo, "Yer taxi's waitin' outside."

In the courtyard is a black prison van. One of the vigilantes opens the back door and says to Mailcoat, "Sir?"

Mailcoat says, indicating the back of the van to the others. "Ya, we'll ride in back. You two guys ride up front. Let's get goin'." They sit on the one bench seat, Mavis in the middle. The van lurches away.

For a while they are silent. Then Mavis says, "I can't thank you enough, JB." Turning to Nimmo she says, "You'll be okay." They can make out through the narrow prison van windows ASP banners and huge posters of the grimacing *Der* Fiddler in his 'fierce and proud' mode festooning every building and many private homes. Also much in evidence are new popular street signs and badges and bumper stickers and T-shirts, broadcasting 'Terminate the enviro-vermin'.

Nimmo says to JB, "Art is a powerful political tool, Mr. Mailcoat. Fred and the Revolution are drilled into the ordinary citizen's consciousness." He pauses and says "Thank you. Where are you taking me?"

Mailcoat stretches a bit on the bench seat, scratches his belly and says, "I sure wish Slick was here. Oh yeah, where we're goin'. East. There's a checkpoint at Bordertown. You'll be home free, back in Candidia."

Nimmo says, "You know if you let me go, I'm going to have to talk about this."

JB says, "The party don't care about what outsiders say. They don't have to."

The rest of the journey proceeds in silence. Eventually the van halts at a bridge and the back doors open. When they step out of the van, Nimmo looks around and sees they are at a brightly lit Alberian border checkpoint. Across the bridge is his safe haven, the Candidian side. Two government officials in plain clothes are waiting there to receive a political refugee.

JB says to Nimmo and Mavis, "Ya better say yer goodbyes."

Mavis reaches into her shirt and gives Nimmo back Tom's notes. She says, "This will help tell your story." He takes them, says nothing, turns, and walks away.

IN THE BACK of the van on the return trip from Bordertown, Mavis says to JB, "Nimmo told me some of the terrible things that have been going on out there. He told me —"

"I know what's happenin' out there, Mave. An' I started it all. Like, I started a monster. It was just the money, Mave. It was just business."

Mavis philosophizes, "In this universe, JB, things are associated. Where there is an action there's a reaction, it's not just all random. Look at the confluence. First the ducks. Then I'm there. It could have been hushed up, but Nimmo and his people were right there too. By the time I saw you, it was all over the place. Listen, JB, you don't need to carry the burden all on your own."

JB says, "I guess nobody started nothin'. It all come together and no good has come of it."

"JB, the ASP revolution has become as toxic as your oilsands. The more productive the oilsands become, the more wealthy and powerful the party, the more bestial the revolution."

JB stifles a sob. "I never thunk it ud come to this, Mave. Who'da ever thought?"

As they bump along, she moves over and puts her hand on his arm. "We can still take the moral high ground JB. We can't stop what's happening but we can try to carry on some of Nimmo's work."

"It's too late for us, Mave, we're in too deep. There ain't nothin' we can do."

"What you think you can't do is walk away from your oilsands. We just have to take the first step."

WALT, FLOSSY, AND CELESTE are gathered around a table at Clobbers, the upscale booze can, knocking back shooters and eating peanuts. Earlier in the night, Walter and Flossy sang duets together on the stage at the Fizzique club including his song *Pussywhipped Me*, only this time with original chord progressions.

"And then you know what that idiot AntiTox creep Vandam yelled at me from the prisoner's box? Can you imagine? *This disgraceful court is a Nazi volksgerichtschof*," laughs Chief Justice Celeste Kinderman to Walter Semchuk. Celeste is ebullient and a bit pissed.

Walt says, "You gotta admit, he went out like a *mensch*. It took balls to yell that when you've just ordered him exterminated. You're embracing this role of a disreputable court."

"Phhht. He was an asshole."

Flossy says, "Well, I feel a bit sorry for Dr.Vandam. He was one of my sessional profs — Ethics of Technology and Culture 101."

Celeste says, "Don't feel sorry for him, they're all traitors."

"The revolution has given you your nasty pills, Celeste," says Walt.

"The nasty pill dispenser was your invention. You and your high-flying girlfriend!" says Celeste.

"You mean my high-flying ex-girlfriend."

Flossy looks with trepidation at the red bowling ball bag at her feet.

Walt carries on, "Celeste, now everything is going swimmingly for the party, the oilsands are going flat out. I can't believe how those FarEaster nuke trucks have ramped up production."

Celeste says, "It's true, then? They're really using those nukes at the sands? Boy, they've gotta watch that stuff if it's the same uranium I was brokering."

"Why is that?" asks Walt, not particularly interested.

"Nah, Let's just leave it. It's late, I've got other things on my mind, why complicate it." She yawns and elects for the existential no choice. She turns, "Well, it's late. Flossy, dear… could you go over and get our coats?" Flossy flounces away from the table but glances back at the bag.

Celeste says in a low voice to Walt, "Have you been out to the Arsehold bunker to check on the gold?"

"I was out there with Baycell Sharpe. It's all there, just as you said."

"My wife doesn't know anything about the gold, by the way."

Flossy returns with their coats. Unsteady on her feet, she is the worse for drink and in a rebellious mood. She lifts the bowling ball bag free from its nest of peanut shells. She hands the bag to Walt and says, "It was in the upside-down Tiffany bowl in the downstairs pole lamp." She thrusts the bag at him and he takes it. Walt knows full well what is in the bag.

Flossy says, "Ursula told me about the gold." Celeste's eyes bug out. "Just when I fired up the chainsaw, she was bawling and everything. She said *don't do it and I'll make you rich.* I said *that's a deal.* She said *there's tons of gold, you can't believe how much.* I said *where.* She told me *the Arsehold bunker.* And then I cut her up." She pouts. "I didn't like her."

When the going gets weird, the weird turn pro.

— Hunter S. Thompson

PART FOUR

————

The Bunker

————

FOURTEEN

AT THE MOMENT, George Bovich is more interested in his bologna sandwich than in the workings of his portable mini-power reactor. He and his buddies call these rolling reactors 'mobile nukes'. There are a bunch of them perched like locusts on the banks of the Athabauna River, superheating the water that separates the oil from the sands. George glances at the master dial. The needle is bouncing back and forth into the red. He puts down his sandwich. Strange, he thinks. He rummages around for the manual. It's all in FarEast, so it's not much help.

"Hey Chip, we got a manual in English?"

Chip crawls out from the back of the truck. "Not that I know of." Pulling his goggles down, he wipes his streaming brow under his hardhat, "Shit, it's awful hot back there all of a sudden."

George radios over to his buddy on the opposite bank. "Hey Charlie, your dials acting up?"

"Yeah, hey, main dial's stuck in the red. Maybe we should call the high-tech guy at the plant. Truck's startin' to shake too."

Bovich looks again at his dial. "Mine's maxed too. And the truck's shakin' like a sonofabitch. Holy shit."

WALT, IN AN INTROSPECTIVE frame of mind, is ensconced in his legislative office, reading *Mineral Collectors Quarterly* and listening to the soaring introduction to Bach's St. John Passion. *This music captures the success of the revolution,* he thinks. He is struck and puts down his journal. The revolution is going beyond all he had anticipated. He shakes his head and smiles, his spirit soaring like a ship's prow rising up after plowing under. *I am once again the captain of my own ship. Pussywhipped no more.* He puts his book down. Now is the time to open Flossy's red leather bowling bag.

As Walt reaches for the zipper on the side of the bowling bag, a horrendous cacophony of sirens and emergency vehicle warning horns erupts. The sounds intensify. Both his cell phone and his desk phone start ringing, then go dead. There is an urgent knock at his door.

"What is it?" he barks.

"Sir! Mr. Semchuk!" Now a frantic pounding on his door.

Walt wrenches the door open. "What the hell?" The intense wailing of multiple police and ambulance and fire sirens persists.

One look at the face of the horrified functionary, an ASP security guard at the legislature, answers his question. He looks past the man and out the high windows over the elaborate carpeted staircase. The whole of the sky is lit up. It is on fire. He gasps, "The whole fucking sky is on fire!"

The guard retreats down to the end of the hall. He huddles in the corner of the corridor, holding himself, pissing himself. The pool spreads at the feet of his ASP cowboy boots.

Walt looks back at the illuminated heavens. He looks long and hard. His emotions drain. Everything that has bolstered him has collapsed. His heart drops right into his balls and he loses himself again.

Containing his emotional shock, he concentrates his mind to go through the motions of survival. He checks his mobile and it is dead, as is the desk telephone in his office. He utilizes the red phone, set on an emergency frequency with its own independent, protected network. Baycell Sharpe, always the consummate professional in any situation, answers.

"Sharpe."

"It's Semchuk."

"They've blown up the sands." Baycell demonstrates his usual flatness of affect.

"They being—?"

"Likely the mobile nuclear reactors."

"That's what I figured. Where are you now?"

"In the underground parkade, sir. Vigilantes are bringing up the emergency fleet. Armed and armoured Land Rovers. Meet me here."

"What about Fred?"

"We're sending a helicopter to his home."

"What about Kinderman? We'd better scoop her. She has certain knowledge. Can you get an order to the Fiddler Youth?"

"Consider it done, sir."

"Thank you." Walt stuffs a few papers into his briefcase and thinks better of it. What the hell, what for? He grabs the bowling bag, and makes for the fire escape stairs that lead down to the legislature's underground private car park. There he locates Baycell with Inspector Luther Ballast of the vigilantes. Baycell is self-contained and in charge. His features are expressionless behind his rimless glasses; his mouth is pinched.

Inspector Ballast snaps to rigid attention and clicks his cowboy boot heels.

"*Heil* Fiddler!"

"Mr. Sharpe."

"At your service, Mr. Semchuk. Inspector Ballast's people have brought up the convoy vehicles."

"Sir. My respectful report, sir. All roads are clogged with pileups of vehicles. There are people fighting, mobs everywhere. Looters are cleaning out stores. Complete chaos. The first responders are overwhelmed. Many are deserting their posts. This is universal, in all centres large and small."

"Your recommendation, Inspector?"

"Helicopters, sir. They've been ordered and on the way from our contingency base."

"Any communication with our main troop placements?" asks Baycell.

"No, sir. Silence on all emergency frequencies, including the fail-safe frequency, sir."

"Ummm. Thank you. Please advise us when you are prepared to evacuate. Mr. Semchuk, I have selected a rendezvous point."

"Let me guess, Mr. Sharpe. The Arsehold Bunker."

CELESTE STEPS OUT her front door and glares at the burning skies. Tyler Rourke is running up her drive with a brace of the Fiddler Youth. They march up to her and raise the *Heil* Fiddler salute.

Tyler says, "Chief Justice, we've been sent here by Mr. Sharpe to protect you. There's real trouble out there in the streets."

Celeste says, "Bring up the limo, right now."

"Where to, ma'am?" Tyler asks.

One of the Fiddler Youth yells out, "We won't be going

nowhere. It's just mobs and looters everywhere."

Celeste screams, "Bring up the limo and that's an order. You'll be taking us to Arsehold."

The youths look at each other incredulously, then turn and walk to the garage.

Flossy boings out the door clutching her shiny polka dot overnight bag as the limo crunches up the gravel driveway. They get in and Celeste orders, "Drive us to Arsehold. Let's go." To Flossy she says, "We've got to get our hands on that gold."

The limo clears the driveway, gets halfway up the block and stops. A solid wall of abandoned vehicles blocks their passage. People are milling about the vehicles, some fighting, some huddled together. The scene is chaotic.

Celeste steps out of the limousine, "Clear the way there. I am the Chief Justice of the Special Peoples' Court." Some men and women clutching broken bottles and clubs move towards her. The three youths are out of the car.

"Fuck you, lady. We're out of here. It's everyone for themselves!" cries Tyler.

Flossy is also out of the car. "Take me with you!" she cries.

Tyler grabs her arm. "Okay, come on babe." They head for the alley.

Celeste holds up her hand. "Halt and disperse or you will spend the night in Lubyanka." Tyler is pulling on Flossy's arms but she looks back. The last image Flossy has of her wife is of her being torn apart by the mob.

FRED, WALT, BAYCELL, AND HAROLD are the ragtag fugitive government-in-exile, holed up in the Arsehold Bunker. They are the only ones there so far, protected by a small group of vigilantes under the command of Inspector Ballast. Fred, looking bedraggled, says to Walt in a rare, lucid moment, "I hope the others make it." Walt shrugs. He is still clutching the bowling bag.

The Arsehold Bunker dates to the sixties. The installation has three levels beneath the former bachelor officers' quarters of the closed air base. Back in the Cold War days, the Alberia government secured and stocked the underground bunker in what they thought was a probable event of nuclear war. It was ready for use at the wail of the first air raid siren. The fugitive government would sit out the apocalypse, govern the province, and lend heart to the masses by messages of hope. Then they would re-emerge when the radiation levels had subsided to tolerable doses, to lead the remnants of the surviving population to greater glories. That was the theory of the bunker.

Fred's fugitive ASP government finds the Bunker still stocked with bottled water, camp bedding, an abundance of tinned and freeze-dried food, hotline telephones, emergency radio broadcasting frequencies, air filters, refrigeration, and a chemical toilet. There are working generators and a deep well. The gold is stashed in a vault three levels down.

On the first level down is a war room of sorts with a huge conference table and wall charts. Here the fugitives confer. Walt is sitting despondently at the end of the table, clutching the bowling bag. Fred is rummaging in the pullout map drawer.

"Well," Harold rationalizes to his companions, "I had a premonition that something big and ugly was coming down the pike. But this whole thing is beyond me."

Baycell, leans over to Harold and says, "We'll survive down here. We are safe and protected." He smiles. "Don't you worry." Then he sits back and folds his hands across his middle as if he is chairing a finance meeting. "Inspector Ballast has briefed me. A nuclear accident detonated at a strategic point in the bitumen archipelago and the chain reaction propelled a firebomb, igniting the entire oilsands." The others shake their heads in wonder. "The devastation and fallout has wiped out the whole area and northern venues are being destroyed in the shock waves. The ignited surface oil has blown up in a wildfire. I managed a phone consultation with one of our energy people just before he was obliterated and in his opinion, the oilsands will burn out of control for a long time."

Fred Fiddler remarks, "I wonder how many ducks up there are dead now?"

Walt replies: "Five hundred million dead ducks, Fred."

Fred frowns over the situation map he has spread over the end of the conference table, striving to appear in charge and decisive. He stabs at a point on the map. "The FarEaster regiment will redeploy to this point." He locates another point on the map, his forefinger stabbing. "The Alberia Security Police will redeploy at this point and disperse to clear rights-of-way to the border." He hunches his shoulders and adopts his trademark scowl. "We are looking for exit points to the Montexia border."

Walt says, "Fred, calm down. There's no FarEaster regiment. We don't have any regiments."

A whirring of a landing helicopter, and JB and Mavis stagger into the war room, disheveled and exhausted. "Jazus Fuckin' Kee-rist, we just got out with our ass an' a gallon a gas, I'll tell ya, hey Mave? What a fuck-up!"

Mavis peels off her jacket, and says, "It's raining black out there."

JB says, "Sheeit, I forgot the dog …. Where do I find a

225

beer?"

The others are relieved about Slick. Harold points at the door. "Kitchen's down the hall, JB." JB gives him a look and says, "Grab me one, Har'ld, will ya. Fer ol' times sake if fer nothin' else."

Baycell says, "Let me help you, Harold."

Mavis says, "Inspector, it looks ugly on the ground. Just what is happening out there?"

Inspector Ballast briefs the newcomers, "The accident chain reaction at the oilsands has the same impact that the detonation of a nuclear warhead would have over that area: the crippling of military and civilian communications, power, transportation, water, food, all amenities, all infrastructure. Thousands of Alberians are dead. Many others will die from the fallout, of starvation, lack of medical care, and violence. Looting will be rife, random violence will be out of control."

Mavis says, "How do you know this?"

"I have this from such operatives as were able to communicate with us up to the blackout."

Harold comes back and hands JB a beer. Baycell has a clipboard on which he has made notes. Harold says, "JB, you'd better make this last, there's only one case. Hope it tastes okay. Problem is ... it's been here for, er, a few years." Baycell adds, ticking off his clipboard, "Supplies are limited, rationing will be imposed."

Mavis says, "Well, we'll make the best of it. It's better in here than it is out there. Tell us more, Inspector." JB smiles at her.

Inspector Ballast continues the briefing. "Displaced persons will be moving in on surviving southern communities. They'll certainly be moving in on us."

Walt adds, "For sure. They'll see our vigilantes and

helicopters and know that someone important is in here."

Baycell says, "The material destruction is beyond severe: it is as if the entire top two-thirds of Alberia has been destroyed by, say, the combination of a massive earthquake and the impact of a rogue asteroid strike."

"Just like when the dinosaurs got wiped out," comments JB, sucking on his precious beer.

Mavis says, "Well, surely it's going to spread into adjacent parts of Candidia."

Walt, not feeling benevolent, snaps, "That's their problem."

"Yes, sir," says Ballast. "There will be small pockets of people who will somehow survive, form communities for protection, rob and plunder each other. Northern Alberia will be a wasteland, for perhaps decades to come."

Mavis exudes a quiet confidence. "What's the prospect of our escape elsewhere?" She's already thinking ahead.

Ballast continues, "Well, ma'am, we have three helicopters standing by. Some fuel is stockpiled here, precious little, in point of fact. Fuel stashes elsewhere are inaccessible in all practicality — they can't be reached at this time – and then they will just disappear with looters and opportunists. There is one vehicle, a Land Rover, rather ancient, stored years ago. The situation is very guarded. Outside, there's societal and economic collapse, massive human casualties, destruction on, well —"

"A demonic scale, is that what you mean to say Inspector?" Mavis contributes. "Thank you for the briefing, Inspector Ballast." She searches her backpack for cigarettes and cannot find them. "Harold, is there any tobacco around?"

Baycell looks down at his inventory list, "No tobacco noted in stores."

Mavis mumbles, "This could be a rough few days."

CD EVANS AND LM SHYBA

Fred straightens catatonically. "For your service to the State, Ballast, you are hereby appointed Air Chief Marshal of the Protectorate. That is my Ordinance."

"Oh, Fred," Walt snaps, his patience with poor Fred's galloping lunacies sorely tried. "Please give it a rest. We don't have an air force. We don't have fuck all."

"The helicopters, sir," says Inspector Ballast.

"And precious little to run them on except hot air."

"Hot air? Good thing Fred's around," JB whispers to Mavis.

Inspector Ballast snaps to attention, clicks his heels, "With your leave, I'll retire to check our perimeter defences. They should hold up. They're double-fence barbed wire with steel stanchions. Our men are armed and well-trained. Message of hope. Confidence is high! *Heil* Fiddler!" Fred returns the ridiculous stiff-armed salute. Inspector Ballast departs. The cold sharp strikes of his steel heel clickers reverberate down the long corridor. There is silence at the table, everyone lost in sober thought. Mavis is dying for a smoke. She wonders what has happened to Nimmo.

OVER THE NEXT FEW DAYS, they settle into their own survival routines. Harold and Baycell construct a miniature golf green in the corner of the war room. JB and Mavis set up a hobby table in the opposite corner and are carving duck decoys out of old airplane wheel chocks. Fred spends most of his time pouring over his collection of maps.

The denizens of the bunker, being fugitives, have dropped their inhibitions, except for Walt. Walt is enervated. He passes his time in a desultory fashion, reading old copies of the *Boys' Own Annual.*

Inspector Ballast does a helicopter overflight of the area confirming his apprehension that bands of starving and desperate scavengers have converged on them.

He reports to the bunker residents: "Their numbers expand daily. There can be only one reason that they are encamped around the premises of this base. They are aware of our presence in this installation. And their numbers, as I say, are growing."

Humming buried generators power the electrical grid for the amenities of the facilities. These are shut down for most hours of the day, as their fuel supplies are dwindling. At the dead of night with the generators stopped save for one backup for emergency lighting, the residents lie awake listening to the unearthly howls and screams of hate and hunger and madness and unspeakable suffering erupting from all about them in the hills surrounding their base.

Baycell and Harold have surrendered to their affinity and are keeping close company. They lie side-by-side, their bodies touching. Harold presses Baycell's hand. In his other hand he cradles his loaded Glock.

OF AN AFTERNOON Walt, hit again with the enormity of the loss of his revolution, chucks his *Boy's Own,* jumps up from his chair and plunges down the staircase clutching his red bowling bag. It has not been out of his sight.

Walt paces the second level corridor leading to the stairs down to the vault. His surrounding are grey, cold, and hideous. Pokey rooms with bunks. No rugs, no decorations and, poor Fred, no mirrors. There are rodent droppings everywhere, bat guano and cobwebs all over the place. It is a desolate prospect. He descends the final moldy set of stairs like an old man.

There are patches of slimy moss on the steep, dirt steps and in the stairwell. When he reaches the vault, he puts down the bowling bag and with both hands grasps the vault door handle, wrenching it down. The heavy door creaks open.

He is hit by a radiant brilliance emanating from massive piles of gold bars. He staggers back and then remembers his bowling bag. With it, he is drawn into the room. Now it's time to open it. He places the bag on top of one of the piles of gold at shoulder height, unzips it, and opens the flap. The eyes of Ursula's severed head are fixed upon him.

Walt, at a loss for words, cribs from Shakespeare. "Alas, poor Ursula! I knew her." His memory carries him back. "All is quite lost. My darling of infinite lust, I loved you and I need you now." He steps back, bereft, horrified at her image. He is drawn back towards her. "Without you, this gold is base coin. I have no purpose. Here hang those lips that I have kissed I know not how oft."

The sound of approaching steps gives him pause. He turns as Baycell enters the vault, all business, brandishing his clipboard.

"Taking inventory, Mr. Semchuk ... Walt?"

Walt reels back in surprise. "First names? Walt it is then, Baycell." He straightens and affects to be all business. "Have you heard from Ballast about the mobs out there? Sooner or later, they'll come after us."

"It's getting scary, Walt." Baycell is staring at Ursula's head, which is staring back at him.

"Well," says Walt, "we can't hold out without troops. What's our vigilante strength?"

"Poor. There have been desertions, of course ... Walt, would you mind turning her head the other way?"

Walt lifts the flap and zips the bag, placing Ursula's head, for the moment, in abeyance. *She needs her queenly crown,* he thinks.

Baycell continues, "Some deserters hope to find loved ones, other guys flee in panic. We are reduced to about seven or so dedicated men-at-arms."

"I see." Walt takes time to contemplate. "I should say it is time for Fred and me to call in some markers, Baycell."

"No time like the present, Walt." Baycell helps himself to a gold bar.

"I've been thinking about this already, Baycell. You know who's surviving out there? The War Bonnet First Nations, that's who. Fred and I have done the tribe some service. Time to contact them."

Back upstairs in the war room, Mavis is saying to JB and Harold, "... and sooner than later, the mobs are going to come after us."

Harold replies, "How the hell are we going to get out of here, Mavis?" He looks around for Baycell.

Mavis says, "I may be able to make good on a favour. You know who's surviving out there? Bikers. I've got an in with the Darktown Riders."

Harold says, "The Darktown Riders?"

Mavis says, "Yup. I've got to figure out how to contact them. I've got to talk to Walt."

JB is silent. He is thinking about his grandkids.

FIFTEEN

MAVIS POUNDS down the stairs of the bunker leading from the war room and runs the length of the corridor separating the narrow bunkrooms from the lavatories. "Walt? Where are you? I think we've got a way out of here!"

Walt slowly ascends the moldy staircase leading from the vault up to the bunk level where he sees Mavis jumping around as if someone's lit a firecracker under her. "I've just come to something like that too, Mavis. Let's talk."

Walt waves over to a lumpy old couch that sags against the concrete wall of the small common area. Mavis springs up and spirals her limber body up against the rickety arm piece, exploding dust all around in swirling patterns. She says, "I know where there are some bikers close by, The Darktown Riders—"

"Hmmmm," interrupts Walt, "valued clients of the firm. I remember when Fred and I—"

"I've got a contact. My friend Kayla is with them. Bikers are mobile, tribal and disciplined. If anyone can get us out of here, they can."

"I'll match you, Mavis. Fred and I did some good work for them and back in the nineties—"

"Walt, listen." She scowls at him. "We need each other. Let's make this a partnership and not a one-up exercise."

Walt sits back, rubs his face. "You're right, Mavis. I'm glad you're making decisions and sharing the responsibility." He doesn't know Mavis well but he's always appreciated her fiery personality and level-headed intelligence.

"Where do you know Kayla from?"

"They were my next-door neighbours. Her boyfriend Mick is the president. They moved out to the compound at Silver Lake some time ago."

"Sounds very promising if we can contact them."

"We can't get them on any cell network … hey, there's a helicopter we can use isn't there?"

"I think so, if there's fuel. Mavis, you know, there's another group that might help us too. The War Bonnet tribe. They're not that far away."

Mavis is excited. "The War Bonnets won the PetroFubar Multicultural Enviro-Fund Contest that I organized for the Bos Taurus rally so I had quite a bit to do with them too. I met the chief. His name is Elvis."

He nods. "Elvis Running Deer. He is a good friend of Fred's and mine."

She starts to get up, "Okay, Walt. Let's call in our favours. We've got to get going on this right away." She settles back down for a moment and looks at him. "You okay? You're looking a bit rough, Walt." She points over to the decrepit staircase. "You seem to spend a lot of time down there."

He says, "Come see." Walt leads the way to the vault.

Mavis follows him down the steep stairs, feeling her way in the dim light. The third level down is dank and forbidding. As he reaches for the vault door, she says, "Is this the dungeon?" She imagines it houses a well-used rack and an iron maiden. Instead, she is amazed to see piles of gold bars.

She steps forward and rubs her hands on the gold, feeling its power. "Well," she says to Walt, "I guess we can buy our way out of here." She turns her hands over and sees sparkling flecks of gold on the palms of her hands. She flashes back to JB's golden duck and the euphoria the gold induced in her then as it does now.

She removes a bar from the pile and says to Walt. "It would be a good idea to demonstrate our solvency to our saviours."

Walt's red bowling bag looms from its perch atop the nearest pile.

BACK IN THE WAR ROOM, they convene a meeting of the bunker residents. Mavis takes charge. She says, "Walt and I have an idea of how we're going to get out of here." She holds up the gold bar.

JB's eye's bug out and his jaw practically hits the floor. "Holy Shit, Mave, where'd that come from?"

"I don't know the whole story but we're sitting on a pile of this. It's down in that moldy dungeon. Back to the idea Walt and I hatched. There are some people we can call on. Inspector Ballast, how are our vigilantes holding out?"

"They're not, ma'am. I'm sorry to report most have defected to the hostiles out there with their weapons. If they had known about the gold, they may not have left."

Baycell queries, "If the hostiles were to move against us?"

Ballast answers, "They'd overwhelm our guards and seal us in this hole. These hostiles are hungry, homeless, and desperate. They'll kill us. We're trapped like rats."

"Like rats!" Harold quails.

JB puffs himself up, "We can hold 'em off like at the Alamo."

Fred leaps up and barks at Ballast, "Field Marshal, call

up the reserve regiment now. That is my order." The others ignore him.

JB hollers, "We got food and water can keep us alive fer weeks and months down here!"

Ballast says, "But there are air vents. If they find them and pipe smoke down, we'll be smoked out."

Mavis yells, "Stop freaking out! Listen up. Walt?"

Walt says, "Inspector, can one of our helicopters make it to the War Bonnet Reserve — relatively close. The foothills west of here. And back?"

"Fuel's short but yes, sir. I'll pilot it myself."

Before she leaves the war room, Mavis whispers over to JB, "Hollow out a couple of your ducks."

"I take yer meanin', Mave."

INSPECTOR BALLAST cranks up the helicopter, a military three-seater, and Mavis and Walt get onboard. As it rises, they observe multiple encampments dotted all around the perimeter of the old air base, smoke rising from fires, various battered forms of transport. Scrofulous hostiles take potshots and hurl threats.

Dense columns of black angry smoke rise from the Bos Taurus city site. The air is acrid and choking. As they rise above the accumulations of smog, the sky above bathes all below in a fierce, unrelenting white light, almost blinding in its intensity. They all don safety goggles.

The helicopter skims over the littered highway west to the reserve lands. It is strewn with derelict vehicles, some overturned, all abandoned and looted. Some poor souls seek shelter in the wrecks. Over the roar of the engine, the occupants shout their conversation.

Mavis says, "Motorcycles can get through there. Tricky but doable. I'm confident bikers'll be the most successful survivors out here."

Walt says, "We're about to drop in on the other most successful survivors."

Ballast says, "We're puttin' her down."

THE OVERHEAD RHYTHMICAL ROAR of the helicopter attracts a surge of War Bonnet tribal members and howling packs of mongrel dogs. As the helicopter descends and hovers over a clearing not far removed from a clutch of dwellings, warriors push back the excited children and step forward. They are all armed with Winchesters and shotguns.

Inspector Ballast pokes a white flag on a pole out his side window port. The warriors stand silently. Walt and Mavis step out, heads down and crouching to the perimeter. Ballast stays at the controls. Walt and Mavis stop, kneel down, and raise their arms to demonstrate that they come in peace.

Walt says, "I come to speak to your Chief."

One of the warriors says, "He's right here." And with that, Elvis Running Deer, traditional plaits bound with buckskin, steps out from the group of warriors. "Hello there, Walt. Oh, and hi, Mavis."

Elvis steps forward and shakes hands with both of them. He leads them out of the range of the helicopter.

To Walt, he says, "Hey, you look the same."

"Same old bastard, Elvis."

"Where's Wise Owl Spirit? Did he make it out alive?"

"Fred is around, but he's a bit, how can I say, out of touch, Elvis. Lots of pressure on the man. How are your people making out?"

"Real good, Walt. Nobody fucks with us." They walk along the dirt path towards the settlement. "We're doin' better than most of them out there."

Mavis says, "Northern Alberia is a wasteland. The oilsands is a serious nuclear fallout zone, but what we have here is a major serious atmospheric disruption with airborne toxins from the sands. That's what this smog is all about."

Elvis asks, "How long is it going to last?"

"It's going to last a long while. The biggest problem is the refugees streaming out of the north and panic in the south."

Walt says, "There's societal breakdown. There's no law and order. There's no food."

Elvis says, "There's still plenty of game out in these parts." He stops and looks at Walt and Mavis. "So, you didn't drop by just to visit. What can we do for you?"

Mavis says, "To start, I sure could use a smoke."

"Sure, here's a cigarette Mavis. In fact, take the whole pack."

Elvis takes a few steps and says, "Let's all walk down to the river."

Walt says, "Times sure change, eh, Elvis."

"For you, not for us. Way before this oilsands disaster, we came back to the land. My people have embraced the old ways," says Elvis. "We didn't even sniff your revolution. We have our own customs and laws. We survive good. And we don't take anythin' more from the land than we need."

They walk along the green riverbank for a while in silence. Mavis flicks her butt into the water and says, "Walt, let's get down to the nuts. Tell Elvis why we're here."

"Wise Owl Spirit and I have a request, Elvis."

"Figured something was coming, Walt. What do you and Fred need?"

"We, that is, the government, such as it is, are holed up and surrounded by hostiles."

"Where?"

"You won't believe it. A former survival bunker on the old air force base. Arsehold."

"No shit, Walt. Good on you guys."

"No shit, Elvis. But our lease is running out. The bad guys are closing in. If we could get here from the bunker, could you put us up for a while and give us sanctuary? I'm thinking from here we try to get across the border to Montexia."

Elvis looks hard at Walt. Then he says, "I don't have a problem with you and Fred, Walt. The tribe owes you, you know that, because of what you and Fred did for the First Nations. But how many are you?"

Mavis says, "There's six of us." She pauses, swings off her backpack and pulls out the gold bar. "We can pay you. We're sitting down in that bunker on a pisspot full of gold."

"Gold?" He stares at the bar in her hand.

Mavis continues, "Real gold, 99 percent pure. It's an old government stash, everybody forgot about."

"So you mean our hospitality would be well rewarded?"

Walt says, "That I can guarantee, if we can get transport."

Elvis reaches into his windbreaker for his cigarettes. Mavis proffers the pack. He lights up. "I can tell you guys, me and my people didn't care much for your dictatorship, but we're obligated to Fred and you, Walt. War Bonnets always honour our obligations, even if it sticks in our craw. Some of us aren't happy about sheltering, well, fascists. Let's call a spade a spade. But …." He shrugs. "That said, a debt's a debt and it's gotta be paid. I guess it don't hurt if my community gets well rewarded."

"You will be, Chief Running Deer," says Mavis.

As they walk back to the helicopter, Walt asks, "Chief, can any of your warriors provide an escort for us from Arsehold?"

Elvis waves at the helicopter, "What's wrong with that thing?"

Walt replies, "There's six of us. We'd have to make three trips. Our fuel situation is bad. We need someone to get us here."

"Nope, Walt. Our warriors are committed to our community. We're not for hire by white guys. I can't send them out to fight hostiles to Arsehold and back. We can't afford to lose any of our fighting men that way."

"That's fair, Chief. Thank you."

Walt and Mavis crawl into the helicopter. Inspector Ballast cranks the machine to life.

Walt asks, "What's the fuel situation, Inspector?"

"After this trip, I'd say critical, sir. We won't be flying anywhere."

Mavis says, "Okay, so let's made the trip back worthwhile. Next stop, the Darktown Riders clubhouse at Silver Lake."

"I hope you know who you're dealing with there, ma'am. Those people are heavy."

"We know who we're dealing with."

At height, they traverse the blighted landscape. They might as well be on the far side of the moon.

INSPECTOR BALLAST puts the helicopter down on the dirt road outside the gate of the heavily armed biker compound. The Darktown Riders clubhouse is a fortress, the outside walls and the roof protected with metal plates. There are sniper holes at points in the walls, the perimeter is surrounded by triple-mounted razor wire, and inside that, a ten-foot security wall is topped with razor wire. High security lights are stuck up on poles. Security cameras pick up all perimeter movement. Two large aerial communication discs project up from the roof. Fierce armed guards patrol inside and outside the perimeter walls and all eyes are on the helicopter as it descends.

A big leather-clad biker bellows through the bullhorn. "Who the hell're you?"

Walt cups his hands, yells, "I'm your lawyer, asshole!"

"Wha…? You some fuckin' asshole yourself? Fuck off, motherfucker."

Out from behind the big biker steps Kayla Vandam. Kayla instructs the biker, "They're cool, Corrector, roll back the gate." He does so. She runs out and embraces Mavis as Walt looks on incredulously.

Mavis, hanging onto Kayla says, "The first thing you've got to know is that Nimmo is safe. They were going to hang him but my boss and I got him out."

"Girlfriend, I am so relieved. We owe you big time."

"Now it's my turn to collect."

Walt looks back and recognizes Mick Beebe, who is striding toward Mavis. He wears a jolly smile and he gives her a big bear hug.

Mick Beebe looks over and recognizes Walt at once. "Holy fucking shitholes, Batman!"

"Hey, Mick, my man."

Mick waves Corrector aside and gestures for Mavis and Walt to enter the compound.

Kayla looks past Mavis at the helicopter. "Who else?"

Mavis says, "Just the pilot. He can stay put with the beast."

Mick says, "We wouldn't mind having that machine."

Walt shrugs, "We'll get to that. If you help us out, you can have it, and a lot besides."

Kayla says, "Yeah? Tell us about it, man. A lot of what?"

There is a pause. Mavis says, "We'll tell you about it."

Mick waves at the door of the compound clubhouse, "So come in, take a load o' shit offa your feet." The interior of the clubhouse is the usual permanent party palace, guys dozing, with a surly looking group playing poker, and large-breasted women cleaning firearms. "There's a whole bunch of us here, Walt. We even got a bunkhouse out back." Mick is talking as he and Kayla lead them to the stairs, and up to an office bedroom in the back. "Have a seat, you guys. Good to see you, like, still alive after all that shit."

Mavis flops down in a chair. Kayla says, "Who's your friend?"

Mick says, "Kayla, this is Walt, the lawyer I told you about. He and his partner Fred saved our ass." He reaches into a bucket and throws a beer to each of them. "What kinda help you want?"

Mavis says, " Fact is, dude, we need your help to get us out of a tight spot."

Mick turns to Walt and says, "I told you, man, I don't forget. We owe you. You want a private army, you got one."

Walt says, "Actually, we do."

Mavis adds, "We're holed up in the old Arsehold air base. You know it?"

Kayla says, "Sure. We heard there were folks holed up there and others on the outside wanting in."

Mavis says, "We're boxed in by scavengers and drifters. There's six of us. We want you to get us through the hostiles and to the War Bonnet reserve."

"We can do that. We're an army, Mave. Who's going to

mess with us?"

"But what's in it for us?" Kayla asks.

Mavis says, "We'll pay you off in gold." She holds up her gold bar. "It's piled up in the bunker."

Kayla smiles, reaches out, and takes the gold bar. "We'll keep this as a down payment. Is this what the hostiles are going after?"

Walt answers, "I don't think anybody knows about the gold—"

Mavis breaks in, "What they do know is what they can see. ASP military helicopters and ASP vigilante guards. Their numbers are growing, the word's out."

Walt takes it up, "And they'll be moving in on us soon. We can't hold out for long. If we do somehow hold out, the Candidian feds are going to be coming down the pike to mop up soon enough and we'll be on our way to the Nuremberg trials, part two."

"Yeah," says Mick, "our people get around. I heard Candidians are setting up refugee camps further south.

Says Walt, "Yes, I rather expected that. Our revolution left a mess and they've got to clean it up."

Kayla says, "We're all outlaws, man. Welcome to the club."

Mick gets up from his chair, saying, "So when do you want us to come get you?"

Walt says, "Well, how can we get word to you when we're ready to move? It may be short notice."

Mavis says, "And the telephones aren't ringing these days. Texting is out."

Mick rises and goes over to a tin trunk in the corner of the room. He pushes miscellaneous articles of clothing off the top of the chest. He opens the lid up, rummages around and removes a number of curious cylinders.

"You know what we use for signals, Walt?"

"No, can't say as I do, Mick."

"Fireworks, man." He grabs something like a pillowcase and drops the cylinders into it. He gives Walt the pillowcase.

Kayla says, "I guess we have an understanding that we'll bring enough of our guys so that me and some of the guys can give you an escort, and the others can take over your bunker and the gold."

Walt adds, "Understanding that the War Bonnet tribe gets a cut of the loot. I gave them my word."

ON THE WAY BACK TO THE BUNKER, Ballast pilots the helicopter over the hostiles' encampments. Mavis makes out details through her binoculars. She gasps and shouts, "Walt, the Land Rover is down there in a ditch, wheels up!" What she sees next grabs her throat—two bodies hanging from makeshift gallows. She recognizes their friends Harold and Baycell, united in death.

SIXTEEN

FRED HAS BEEN STUCK for the last month with the others in the Arsehold bunker eating dry biscuits, watching old spaghetti Westerns when the generator is running, and playing checkers with Walt by candlelight when it is not. Now Walt has gone somewhere and Fred feels the need to feed his wounded ego. He pulls out his pocket mirror, sees the deterioration of his noble features, and gasps. His face has sagged, his eyes are dull, his nose is red and runny. His hair has gone white. Fred has a continuing dialogue with himself, out loud. "What a toll public office has taken upon the Lord Protector. Where are the others when the Lord Protector is stuck in this goddamn hole?"

He hears the noises of the gathering forces outside the compound and the sounds start to rouse his passions. He hunches his shoulders, narrows his eyes, and lowers his brows. "I hear the Lord Protector's people. They want to see, they want to hear the Lord Protector."

He goes to his room and dresses himself with particular punctilio — the classic black suit with the clean white shirt, the ASP tie, his shiny black shoes, now scuffed. He scowls at his shoes and rubs at them with a rag. *That's better.* He takes his Napoleon hat from its perch and places it on his head. He tucks his telescope under his arm.

All bluster, he marches up the stairs to the roof. In the distance, he sees a mass of people and he relives the Sunken Coulee rally. In his crazed mind, he sees ASP familiars, the Inner Circle, the magnificent seven, Walt and Ursula and his adoring crowds. The hostiles who are really there are the dispossessed, the desperate, a crew of violent eco-zealots, aimless youth, and a disillusioned Tyler Rourke with his ASP issue rifle.

Fred raises his arms, posing like an extravagant peacock, and launches into the rhetoric of the revolution, The Big Lie. "Citizens, we're taking Alberia out. We've had a bellyful of those Eastern bastards shutting the oilsands down over a bunch of dead ducks."

Tyler takes aim and fires.

THE HELICOPTER carrying Mavis and Walt has hardly touched down and JB is right there gesticulating, oblivious to the still-whirling blades, as they alight from the aircraft. Dust and tumbleweeds fly in all directions. He looks harassed and disheveled. He blurts out, "Fred's down!"

Mavis rushes up to him. "Fred? Down? What happened, JB? Now calm down and tell us what happened." Walt and Ballast stand by.

"Cn ya b'lieve it, Mave, that crazy sombitch got up on th' roof, high noon, hot as hades, and he started givin' a speech. *I must address my people*, that sorta shit. He's outta th' war room an' headin' fer th' stairs, he's wearin' that goofy hat an' wavin' his goofball telescope, Kee-rist! I run up after him, he's out an' raisin' his hand in the air like he's God or somethin', callin' out to th' hostiles. Me, I'm stickin' m' head out th' canopy, prayin' not t' get it shot off. I say *Fred, for Chrissake, step down. There's snipers out there.* Bang. Right like that, an' Fred's down. I'm yellin' somethin' fierce fer Sharpe an' Harold. Nobody comes. Shee-it. I crawl out there and Fred's been shot in th' gut, it looks real bad, blood everwhere. I got him down. Somehow." He stops, overcome. Mavis puts her hand on his arm. Walt's eyes are wide. "If that ain't enough, I go lookin' fer Baycell an' Har'ld. Nowheres. I don' know what t' do with Fred. I cain't put a turnkey on his stomach."

Walt yells out to JB, "Where the hell is he now?"

"He's on the floor in the war room." Walt rushes off to be with Fred.

"JB, we saw Baycell and Harold on the way in. They must have made a run for it. They're done for."

"Aw, them poor bastards. What did they do to 'em?"

Ballast says, "They strung them up, sir."

JB rallies himself and says to Ballast, "I guess we better check the defenses." Mavis heads to the war room to help Walt with Fred. JB and Ballast don body armour for a circuit of their sparsely guarded double barbed wire perimeter. Inspector Ballast greets the vigilante men-at-arms at the barricades. Only three of them remain. "Any complaints, men? Grub okay?" They grunt, salute and parrot, "*Heil* Fiddler!"

Ballast addresses his troops. "Thank you for your continued loyalty and your conspicuous service to the State."

FRED IS IN SHOCK. His clothing is torn open and he is bleeding from his torso wound and from the mouth. Walt and Mavis heave Fred up and spread him out on the map table. Mavis locates the medicine chest stuffed with mysterious bottles, tubes, and dressings. She rips the paper covering off a syringe and says, "Let me handle this. I took EMS training as part of my post-doc in Tapperlite." She fills the syringe with a vial of something and injects the needle into Fred's arm. "Morphine. I think," she says.

Mavis leans forward over Fred and takes his hand. "It's okay, Fred, Walt and I are here." She whispers to Walt, "He's dying."

Walt, choked up, hovers over his old partner. Fred's breathing is shallow but he opens his eyes. "We showed 'em, didn't we Walt?"

Walt is immeasurably sad. He knows they haven't shown anybody anything except excess and failure. But he says, taking Fred's hand, "We sure did, Fred. You were the greatest Lord Protector ever."

Fred gasps a few last breaths and dies. Mavis places a cloth over his face.

JB and Ballast come in from their inspection and Mavis says to JB, "Fred's gone."

Walt, not knowing what to say, utters a kind of eulogy. "We will have to leave Fred's reincarnation to the fates. Only God knows what sort of karmic punishment he's going to get in the hereafter. Maybe he'll come back as a different person, a better person?"

JB says, "He'll prob'ly come back as a cockroach." Then to Mavis he says, quietly, "I'm wonderin' what I'm comin' back as. I started all this."

Walt says to Ballast. "I think, Inspector, that we should not leave the Lord Protector's remains to coagulate."

"I agree, sir. What would you like me to do?"

"I would suggest a suitable immolation, Inspector. There's enough gasoline left?"

"Yes, sir."

"No remains."

AFTER THE BURNING of the funeral pyre that evening, reminiscent of a Viking ritual, Walt retraces his steps to the vault with some trepidation. He is drawn there because when he is not there, Ursula's severed head haunts him. When he is there, she torments him. Now he hopes she will bring him some comfort because he has just lost his best friend. He unzips the bag and pulls down the flap. Ursula's accusing eyes are still staring. They pierce his soul. They will be fixed on him on his descent to hell. He is confronted by her grin. Sitting beside the bag on top of the pile of gold is the partially fashioned gold crown he has been working on, with some vague notion of attaching it to her skull. His real purpose, he rationalizes, is to have final communion with her and say goodbye, take the dreadful severed head in its blood-red bag, and chuck it on the garbage heap. He knows he will not be able to do this. He knows he must take her with him.

He speaks to her as if she were alive. "Should I go with them or end it all here? Paradise is looking rather attractive right now to this fallen architect of the revolution."

She stares at him.

In his mind, she calls to him in soft tones, *Vlad take me.* This returns him to her lustful, silky bed and their matched bodies achieving revolutionary orgasm. He whispers to her, "It was the gold you were interested in all along, Professor Vere, and I'm afraid now we're going to lose it. It's time for us to go, dear. I have an obligation to the others."

He puts the flap up over her face and zips up the bag. He hefts the bag, looks back at the gold, and at the last minute, takes a gold bar. He ascends the moldy staircase and puts the bag and the gold into his room.

Now there are drums beating, as they have been, day and night. Hideous whoops and shrieks sound from close in to the perimeter. Through his night-scope binoculars, Inspector Ballast makes out a number of hostile encampments. "Like stray dogs, ma'am."

Mavis rejoins, "Like hungry wolves."

Walt joins the others. "Well, it's time we fire off the flares. Time is running out. They'll be on us tomorrow, maybe even later tonight." Walt and Mavis take time to talk to Inspector Ballast.

"What of me and my men, Mr. Semchuk?"

Walt looks both grave and concerned. "Tomorrow, Inspector, this place will be under new management. We've spoken to them. Their principal concern is with the gold, and not with our welfare. The Darktown Riders Motorcycle Club will inherit the precious metal that we have been sitting on. That's the price we pay for our lives. Your bottom line is, you and your remaining lads get to live and you get to leave. But not with any of their booty."

"Where should we go, sir? We still serve the state."

"The ain't no more state to serve, Inspector. Look to yourselves. The deal is that the bikers will let you depart unharmed and unmolested. But don't try to smuggle out any of the gold. The bikers will kill you on the spot. Over there…" Walt points to the base of the main stanchion supporting the perimeter fence.

"Yessir?"

"Under that spot, Mr. Sharpe and I took the precaution, some time back, of burying a sturdy bag of gold, deep. In due course, perhaps, you and some of your lads can come back for it. For now, I should give it a wide margin."

"Thank you, Mr. Semchuk."

"You'll have to get out through the hostiles, but some of the bikers will escort you through their lines, and then cut you loose. Nobody is going to challenge the Darktown Riders, unless they're insane. Then, I suggest you head for the refugee camps in the south."

"We all have the ASP police service tattoo, sir."

"Then you may be wise to resign your commission, Inspector, and take the identification documents of one of your dead lower ranks. Then it's just a gaggle of former junior cops staggering out of the wasteland, like any other refugees."

"We'll do our best, sir."

"I'm sure you will. Good luck, Inspector."

Click! "*Heil* Fiddler!"

"I'd be ditching the salute, the slogan and the jackboots, Inspector, as have we all. Perhaps running shoes and ordinary unobtrusive gear? You don't want to be attracting attention to yourselves."

"Sir."

Walt and Mavis confer with JB. They are sitting at a table in the kitchen area. Walt pours them the last of the whiskey in stock. "We'll be out of here tomorrow, I expect, JB," says Walt.

JB grunts. "Yeah? Cain't be too soon fer me, Walt."

Walt says, "JB, assuming we get to the reserve, our tenure there is on sufferance and limited. We'll be carrying gold to pay the War Bonnet tribe, but now is the time to be thinking of our next move from there, because we're going to have to move on."

"Yeah. So what you got in mind, Walt?"

"I have, we have, got Montexia in mind, JB."

"You get us t' th' border an' I'll do th' rest, Walt."

"Let's get packed up. Travel light."

Walt leaves the war room and heads for his room. As he packs, he is overcome by a surge of acrid smoke that in the dim fluorescent light of the second floor corridor can be seen pouring out of a wall air vent. He stumbles, falls to his knees, choking. He hears Mavis calling his name, "Walt, where are you? Walt?" He staggers on his hands and knees up the corridor, clutching the bowling bag.

Mavis collides with him. "Smoke bomb!" she cries. They are both gagging in the thick poisonous fumes. Calling on her cold nerves and presence of mind, Mavis grabs the bag from his grasp and rams it and its death head cargo into the smoke-emitting air vent. With a *ker-schlock*, the soft folds of the bag plug the hole and stop the smoke. She grasps Walt by the arm and pulls him down the corridor into the stairs. They make the war room. They hear the sharp reports of discharging weapons, then it is quiet, save for Walt's and Mavis' retching and coughing.

There is a sharp sound of steel heel clickers on the stairs from the first level, and Inspection Ballast enters the war room. "Hostiles, sir. Couple of them got under the fence and lobbed a smoke bomb into the vent. We shot them."

That night, a moonless night, Walt treats the inmates to a firework display. They enjoy the bursting of multicolored fluorescent plumes curling and spiralling down from their explosion points, wave after wave, until the contents of Mick Beebe's cylinders are exhausted.

THE NEXT DAY, in the glaring light of the merciless sun with no overhead protection save passing clouds of smoke, the bunker dwellers make out the great clouds of dust rising above the formation of motorcycle riders heading towards the bunker. They also hear the sounds of discharging firearms, no doubt from the bikers discouraging hostiles and putting them to rout. Ballast opens the gate. The formidable entourage blasts and roars past the perimeters into the compound, circles in a disciplined arc led by Mick Beebe and Kayla Vandam, and comes to a halt before the bunker building.

JB says, "Shee-it, Mave, these are our saviours?"

"JB, they're the only saviours we've got."

The sight they see is extraordinary and intimidating: rippling-muscled men and women, stone bald or Iroquois hairdos, elaborate tattoos, facial scars and piercings, outfitted cap-a-pie in black leathers, sleeveless sweatshirts and vests, bracelets, armbands, wristbands, all bristling with spikes, gloved and booted, Bowie or Buck knives and pistols and clubs, sawed-off shotguns or rifles in breakaway holsters, warlike and lethal.

The survivors greet their visitors. Kayla dismounts and walks over to Mavis. She gives her a hug and says, "You're riding back of me. So, where is the gold?"

Mick and Corrector, his second in command, waste no time in deploying their troops around the perimeter. The presence of the fierce retinue has its effect. The noise from the hinterland dies. All of a sudden it is quiet. Walt takes Mick and Kayla down to the bunker vault.

While the others are checking out the gold, Mavis leans up to JB and asks, "Did you stick some gold in the bottoms of our ducks?"

"You bet. It's all taken care of, Mave. Like smugglin' a gun in a book." JB points at Mick's bike and says, "I ain't never ridden on one o' these."

"You'll be fine, JB. Just lean back and think of Montexia."

On her return from the vault, Kayla smiles, saying to her people, "Here's the treasurer's report. Yup, it's all there like they said. There's piles of it."

"Listen up," says Mick. "First we're going to load the

saddlebags with the gold for the War Bonnet tribe. Next, Corrector and half of you are going to take over the bunker and hold the place. After we've gone, Corrector will send some of you to take those guys over there...." He points at Ballast and the three troopers, "through the hostile lines, the rest of us are headin' for the reserve."

Walt, Mavis and JB stand by, each with a backpack, waiting to leave. Relays of bikers fill every available escort's saddlebag with gold bars. Mick asks Walt, "I thought there were six of you?"

Walt says, "When we saw you out at Silver Lake, there were six. Now we're down to three. Fred's dead and two others made a run for it and the hostiles got them. We're obliged to you. I expect we'll be doing some hard travelling."

Mick confers with Corrector then mounts his bike at the head of the column. Mavis follows Kayla to her bike and just before they mount, Kayla turns to Mavis and takes off her necklace — a beautiful smoky quartz crystal hanging from a soft leather thong. Kayla says, "Nimmo gave this to me and he'd want me to pass it along to you." Mavis accepts it in silence.

The escort bikers all mount and fire up their fearsome machines. As they separate to mount behind a biker, Walt says to JB, "Any person seeing this blood-stopping sight and hearing this blood-curdling sound is minded to get out of the way, and keep his head down or he's going to lose it."

Kayla says, "Let's ride!"

JB mounts up behind a stalwart rider. He says "Do I get a parachute?" The rider tells him, "You just hang onto my belt, man, and hang onto your ass."

Mick and Kayla lead two lines of leather-clad riders out of the compound. They speed up as they bump and weave and grind over the rough ground in order to make the road. As they attain one rise, a motley collection of scavengers scatters into adjoining deadfall.

The procession departs.

WALT, JB, AND MAVIS meet with the War Bonnet Tribe Chief and Council in their lodge. Walt begins, "Chief and Council, we appreciate that we are guests on sufferance of the tribe."

Elvis interrupts. "So long as you are our guests, Walt, no harm will come to you and your friends."

"We appreciate that, Chief Running Deer. We have a modest proposal." Walt pauses. "We should like to cross the border into Montexia. Montexia is Mr. Mailcoat's home country. We cannot stay in Alberia, and we do not expect your hospitality to be open-ended."

One of the councillors speaks. "It won't be long before some white guys in uniforms come sniffing around, looking for you guys."

Walt says, "We were elected in a fair and free election, like Chief and Council here."

Another councillor says, "Well, now you're in exile and on the run. We're not."

Walt continues. "We are aware of that." He changes the subject. "Except for isolated pockets of civilization — here, for example — the situation in this area is grim. Mavis?" He nods to her.

"Chief and Council, thank you. Our biker escort has brought us straight from the Arsehold bunker to here. Their leader told us that they have been picking up isolated emergency broadcasts."

"Yeah, their leader shared some of that information with

us too, when he got you here," says Elvis.

"We understand that right after the blast, the Montexia-Alberia border was sealed," says Mavis. "And all mountain passes providing passage to the west are barricaded. Our borders with Saskabush are patrolled by Candidian federal police. We're boxed in. Candidians and Montexians are both keeping refugees out."

Elvis holds up his hand. "Well, we don't want our tribe to be in the glue for sheltering you guys. So what's your proposal?"

Walt responds, "You have your payment that the bikers brought with us. We need to get to Montexia. Mr. Mailcoat knows the border well. The border is heavily patrolled, but he tells us it is porous through the Glacierton Evergreen National Park wilderness areas."

"No one can police that whole thing, not around there," says JB, "You get us to th' border, I can git us across, and I'll look after us when we git there."

"Our reserve extends to the border, our sister tribe is on the other side. This is our land. We never surrendered it."

"That makes it easier," says Mavis.

"Yeah, that's all good," says the Chief, "but how d'you propose to get there?"

Walt says, "We camp it overland, staying close within the front ranges, on horseback. With an escort."

The councillors look at each other. Elvis asks, "And where do you get the horses and the escort?"

Walt scrapes back his chair and rises. "Look, with all due respect, Chief, we have paid you handsomely. Face it, you owe us at least an escort to the border."

JB also rises and says, "All we're talkin' about is a couple of your warriors and a horse wrangler."

Elvis says, "The chief and council will deliberate." As Mavis, JB, and Walt leave the lodge, he throws Mavis a pack of cigarettes.

They step out into the grassy field to a chorus of barking from the mongrel dog pack. Mavis lights up a cigarette and takes a deep drag. Some of the dogs come roaring over foraging for food. A yellow Lab-like bitch sniffs around JB and sits down at his feet.

"Hey, what's your name?" He reaches down to scratch her behind the ear but she bites his boot. "Ya might be a hunter. Okay if I call ya Slick?"

Elvis comes to the door of the lodge and says, "We're ready." The dog runs back to the pack.

They go back in and Elvis says, "We're agreed. You get your escort."

As the trekking party makes ready over the next couple of days, Mavis and JB have occasion to stroll together along the river and down to the pond. "Nothin' stays the same, hey, Mave? Nobody stays the same. Look at us now. Think of us then. In some ways it don't add up and in other ways, it makes sense." He shrugs, "I guess."

Mavis takes his arm. "We have much to atone for, JB, but let's do our best to make it good. I don't know about Walt."

"I don't know what's gonna happen to him. He's gonna have to live with himself, Mave."

Mavis rubs her smoky quartz talisman and holds it to her heart. Remembering how Walt admired it, she thinks about gifting it to him to help mend his soul but decides to keep it instead. She takes a deep breath, tips back her head, and lets the chinook wind ruffle through her hair.

MAVIS, JB, AND WALT are escorted by Elvis's cousin, an experienced wrangler and outdoorsman, along with two armed warriors. They are well-mounted on agile mustangs with two packhorses. As they ride past the settlement and out toward the ridge, Elvis Running Deer raises his hand in good-bye. A group of happy children and the pack of barking dogs follow them for a while. From the pack of dogs, the yellow Lab bitch breaks away, runs up to the riders and starts following JB's horse. A boy whistles the dog back. JB turns his horse, gives it the heel and gallops back to the boy.

"That yer dog?"

The boy says, "Well, not really. I sort of look after her."

"Can she come with me? I'll look after her good."

The boy hesitates and says, "Sure, sure, mister."

JB reaches into his saddlebag and takes hold of his duck decoy. He removes the gold brick from its underside, dropping the brick back into his saddlebag. He reaches down and gives the duck to the boy.

"Here. If ya put 'im in the pond, he'll float."

Acknowledgements

CD: I thank first and foremost, mere words inadequate, my co-author and best friend the brilliant Lorene Shyba; for masterfully illuminating our creations, Maxwell Théroux; for perceptive invigilation of the creative process, Rona Altrows and Austin Andrews; for assisting with myriad aspects of care and feeding of the work, Hon. Allan Wachowich QC, LL.D, Allan Shewchuk QC, Laura Stevens QC, Brian Beresh QC, Gillian Marriott QC, Brad Dunne, Michael Hare, Barb Levenick, Jana Rieger, Christel McAndrews, Rob Young; for unfailing moral and advisory support, Kathleen van Mourik, John Martland QC, Hilda and Lenny Smith, Terra Nicolay, Frank Dabbs. I particularly acknowledge the instructive scholarship of Alan Bullock and George Orwell.

Lorene: I am indebted to more people than can be imagined. As far as the book goes, I thank CD Evans and Maxwell Théroux for their fascinating and hilarious collaboration. Big thanks also to Rona Altrows and Austin Andrews who have been sometimes kind and sometimes cruel with their suggestions and analyses but have made *Ducks* a better read, I'm sure. People who have inspired and supported me through this adventure of wordsmithery include: Warwick Andrews, Marcel Bitea, David Bunnell, Barbara Bergen, Brenda Shyba, Jim Parker and Katrin Becker, Kathleen Foreman, Clem Martini, Paul Lawnikanis, Lori Stiffer, Jeff Johnson, Jack, Carolyn and Maddie Shyba, The Rose and Fries clans, the spirits of Paul Andrews, Elsie and Walter Shyba, Larissa Boggs Faulkner, Ruth Simons, Betty Latimer, Shannon Jaeger, Chris Danielson, Marilyn Jesmain, Scott Beach, Heather Elton, Pep Guardiola and FC Barcelona, and every one of my Facebook friends. Finally, a special thanks to my fine colleagues and students at Montana Tech including Chad Okrusch, Pat Munday, Heather Shearer, Henrietta Shirk, and Kay Eccleston. Butte, America is an American experience like no other.

OTHER TITLES

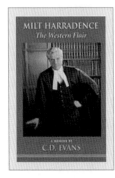

Milt Harradence: The Western Flair

In Milt Harradence: The Western Flair, C.D.
Evans perpetuates the legend of his flamboyant,
larger-than-life colleague with whom he shared
thrills, spills, brilliant courtroom spars — and close
friendship — for over thirty years. According to
Evans, "Yes, there are many fine criminal lawyers
but next to Milt we're all a bunch of soda jerks. He
was the Einstein of barristers and the rest of us
mere Neanderthals."
In addition to painting a portrait of his friend, mentor and benefactor, in
the book C.D. Evans also provides revealing insights into not only the
practice, the events and the characters of the Alberta Criminal Bar.

Price: $30.00 (Canada and USA), Publication Date: 2002; 334 pages; 16
pages of colour photos
Designed and edited by Lori Shyba
ISBN: 0-9689754-0-2

DURANCE VILE
PUBLICATIONS